Finding the Way

Finding the Way

Barbara Yoder

Printed in Canada

Publishing services by Selah Publishing Group, LLC, Arizona.
The views expressed or implied in this work do not necessarily
reflect those of Selah Publishing Group.

ISBN 1-58930-051-3
Library of Congress Control Number: 2001099348

Acknowledgements

Thank you to my husband the love of my life for all his support and encouragement.

To my three beautiful children, my inspiration.

To my sister Kathryn for doing my housework while I wrote.

To my dear friend Lauri for helping me with this book and teaching me so much about writing..

To my best friend Kristen for always being there.

Chapter One

Fourteen-year-old Elizabeth Hostetler settled back in her seat, trying to block out the noise coming from the forty or so other kids still on the bus. Now that her best friend, Rachel, had gotten off, Elizabeth wanted to finish reading her book. She loved to read, but she knew that once she arrived home there'd be no time until after supper. The routine was always the same—arrive home, change her clothes, grab a snack, and begin the evening farm chores.

Sometimes Elizabeth daydreamed of what life was like for her friend Jill. Jill was her next-door neighbor and not Amish. She had no farm chores, just homework, then supper, and the remainder of the evening to read. The thought of being able to curl up with her favorite books to read for a whole evening with no chores made Elizabeth smile. That would be the life, she thought.

But the daydream quickly faded as the bus chugged to a stop at the end of their lane. Grabbing her lunch pail and books she hurried off the bus.

The smell of cookies baking greeted Elizabeth at the door. Hanging her coat and bonnet in the hall closet, she hurried into the kitchen.

"How was school today?" her mom asked. "Learn anything new?"

Elizabeth shook her head, her mouth full of a warm molasses cookie.

"Now don't eat too many," scolded Mom, "and hurry up and get your chores done. We are invited out for supper tonight."

"Where to?" Elizabeth asked, as she glanced through the mail.

"To Daniel and Anna's. It's Daniel's birthday and Anna invited us to a surprise birthday supper."

Daniel was Elizabeth's brother, the oldest of the six Hostetler children. Elizabeth was the youngest , with another brother—Leroy—and three sisters—Marilyn, Linda, and Dena—sandwiched between them.

Daniel and his wife Anna had begun their own family on a little farm several miles away. They now had two little boys, Bennie and Chris, and a recent addition, a baby girl named Elaine.

Elizabeth finished her second cookie upstairs as she changed her clothes. When she reached the barn several minutes later, her brother Leroy and sister Marilyn had already started with the milking.

"Come on, slowpoke," teased Leroy. "Dad has already done your other chores."

"Why do you think I waited so long to come out and help?" laughed Elizabeth, before sitting down beside the last cow waiting to be milked.

"You can finish the chores while I go in to get dressed," said Marilyn. "And don't forget to sweep the milk house when you're done. You forgot the last time."

"If you're so worried that it needs to be done, you do it," Elizabeth told her. Marilyn irritated her. She was always so bossy.

"I've already done your share of the chores tonight," replied Marilyn, stalking out of the milk house.

"Why does she have to be that way?" Elizabeth muttered under her breath. "She's only two years older than me. That shouldn't make her the boss of me." But Elizabeth knew better than to complain to Mom. Mom would just tell her not to argue and to do as she was told. "Oh well," she said to herself, "I'd better hurry or I'll be late."

Back in their bedroom, Elizabeth watched as her sister slipped a dark green dress over her head.

"Is that new?" she asked.

"Yes," answered Marilyn. "It's the one Daniel and Anna gave me for helping out when Elaine was born."

"Where's Linda?" asked Elizabeth, referring to their older sister.

"She went over to their house to help Anna with supper."

"How many will be there?" asked Elizabeth. "I thought we were the only ones going."

It turned out that Anna had invited her family too. So Elizabeth knew she would be glad for any help she could get with all the work of making supper, plus taking care of their three little children.

"Better hurry," Marilyn reminded her. "Dad and Mom are probably ready to go."

Elizabeth carefully pinned her white head covering on her wavy black hair, taking a moment to check her reflection in the mirror. Her dark brown eyes stared back at her. She adjusted her apron to her slim figure. Elizabeth knew her mom said that people shouldn't set store in their looks and to be thankful for how the good Lord made them. But, just the same, Elizabeth wished she had pretty blonde hair and blue eyes like her best friend Rachel.

"Quit spending so much time admiring yourself," Marilyn scolded her again."

Just then their mother called up the stairs telling them to hurry or they would be late. Elizabeth bit back a sharp reply to Marilyn's accusation. It would only serve to get her in trouble. She hurriedly finished dressing, ran down the stairs, and into the buggy. She would ride with her parents as was the custom among the Amish people for younger children. Sixteen was the age to join the youth group or, as they called them, "youngie."

Elizabeth relaxed back against the seat, glad they were using the top buggy tonight instead of the open one. Even though it was April, the night air was chilly but she enjoyed the long buggy ride and the rhythmic clip-clop of the horses' hooves. She wished she could have brought a book along but Dad said it wasn't necessary. Buggy rides were a time for family, a time to meditate and enjoy God's creation.

Elizabeth's thoughts wandered back to the past week when Mom's sisters from out of state were here. Aunt Millie thought Elizabeth was sixteen already. She wished she were; maybe then she could have a little more freedom—like wearing her dresses shorter the way her sister Linda did. But she knew her parents wouldn't approve of that. Dad always said that whatever was in your heart showed by the clothes you wore. Elizabeth wasn't sure about that. She knew that pride was wrong, but was it wrong to want to look nice? Oh well, she was only going to be fifteen on her next birthday in June, so there was no use thinking such thoughts. Besides Mom was always telling her: "Don't wish your life away; it'll go by fast enough."

Elizabeth sighed as she watched the sun sink behind the Pennsylvania hills. Spring was her favorite time of the year, and this year was special. Her school days were almost over. After that her life would begin to change. No more being a carefree schoolgirl, no more seeing her best friend Rachel everyday. Elizabeth wished she could go on to high school, but that would be unheard of as the Amish only go through the eighth grade. Surely there was much more she could learn. She could become a nurse, or learn another language. Maybe she could learn French. After all, some of her ancestors came from France. Mom said her grandpa spoke French and German.

"Looks like we're the first ones here," said Mom, interrupting Elizabeth's train of thought as they turned into the lane.

"Good, that way I can be the first to hold baby Elaine." Elizabeth hopped off the buggy.

"We'll see," smiled Mom as they entered the little screen porch.

"It sure smells good in here," said Mom as they entered the little screen porch.

"Wow, Anna, you even made ice cream!" said Elizabeth, spotting the ice cream freezer in the corner.

"Yes, it's strawberry," said Anna, "Daniel's favorite."

"Where's the baby?" asked Elizabeth, looking around.

"I just put her in her baby seat in the living room."

"Well, I think Grandma should get the first turn," Mom insisted as she picked up baby Elaine.

"Okay, but I'm next!" Elizabeth said.

"Dena is here, Elizabeth," Linda called out from the kitchen where she was washing dishes. "You can go out and bring their baby in, and then you and Mom will both have a baby to hold."

Elizabeth hurried out to help her older sister into the house with her two little boys.

"Hi there," Dena greeted Elizabeth as she lifted four-week-old Justin out of the buggy.

Their mother smiled as she watched them coming up the walk. "Yah, God has been good to us," she mused, "blessing us with six children and now with five grandchildren."

Just as they entered the house both boys began crying at once.

"Come here and tell Grandma what's wrong," Mom made room for two-year-old Solomon on her lap. How she enjoyed her family! It seemed like such a short time ago that she and David were young parents, and now their youngest was almost fifteen.

"This is the life, huh, Mom?" asked Daniel smiling fondly at his mother holding the little ones on her lap.

"Yah, it sure is," she agreed. "I was just thinking that it doesn't seem that long ago when Dad and I were your age."

"Yes, that's right," agreed their father, taking Solomon from her lap. "Enjoy these years, they go by so fast."

Dad's words of advice were cut short by the arrival of Anna's family—a clan of six brothers and four sisters. A wave of noise and excitement accompanied them as they entered the house, filling it to capacity, everyone talking, laughing and fussing over the baby.

"Supper is ready," announced Anna. "Let's go eat."

The crowd migrated toward the dining room and everyone hurried to find a seat around the table.

Daniel waited for the confusion to abate, before asking everyone to bow their heads and say grace. Then, one by one the steaming hot dishes were passed—mashed potatoes, gravy, meatloaf, corn, homemade bread, and jam—food Anna and Linda had worked hard all day to prepare.

"My, you have sure outdone yourself," said Daniel smiling fondly at his wife. "Everything is delicious."

"Yes, it sure is," the family echoed Daniel's praise.

"I want this meatloaf recipe," said Dena.

Elizabeth listened as the adults talked about everything from the weather, to the price of eggs. How different Anna's family was from her own, she thought. They were definitely quieter.

She glanced up from her plate to find Anna's seventeen-year-old brother Matthew watching her. As their eyes met, he mischievously winked at her.

Elizabeth's face reddened and she quickly looked away. How dare he! Why he probably doesn't even know my name, let alone my age. She wished she hadn't blushed.

Matthew smiled to himself as he watched her. She looked cute when she blushed, he thought. I wonder how old she is. Ah well, girls were fun to tease but not to be serious about. He turned his attention back to his plate.

As soon as supper was over and dishes were washed, Daniel brought out a stack of board games—Monopoly, Aggravation, Clue, and checkers.

Elizabeth loved to play games. They—along with her books—helped to pass the long winter nights as, in Amish homes, there were no televisions or radios for entertainment.

"I'll challenge you to a game of checkers, Elizabeth," called Leroy.

"Are you sure you are up to it?" laughed Elizabeth. Even though Leroy was five years older, she could still sometimes beat him at checkers.

"Let's just get started before you chicken out of it," he answered.

Elizabeth sat down, trying hard to concentrate on every move, liking the competition.

"I win!" she announced smugly as she took Leroy's last checker.

"Oh no," he groaned. "I'll never hear the last of this."

"We could make a deal that if you do my share of the milking tomorrow morning, I'll keep this just between the two of us," Elizabeth suggested, laughing.

"I think she got you this time," said Linda.

Leroy laughed. His little sister sure did have a lot of spunk, except that she wasn't so little

anymore. She was beginning to look like quite the young lady. He had witnessed the exchange between her and Matthew earlier at the dinner table and had seen Elizabeth's face turn red as her brown eyes glared at Matthew. She'll do well to keep boys at arms' length at least a few more years, he thought to himself.

Chapter Two

"Elizabeth!" Mom called." Time to get up."

Elizabeth rolled over and looked at the alarm clock. Five-thirty! Surely it couldn't be time to get up yet. Then she remembered, it was Sunday morning and the chores had to be done earlier to get to church on time. She rubbed her eyes sleepily. Maybe she could snooze for just five more minutes.

"Elizabeth!" Mom called a second time. This time her tone was impatient.

"Yes, Mom," Elizabeth answered, jumping out of bed. She hurriedly got dressed and joined Dad and Leroy in the barn. It wouldn't do to be late for church. Today the service was at Rachel's house.

As soon as chores were done and breakfast was over, Elizabeth hurried upstairs to her room to get ready. Carefully she slipped on her navy blue dress, then pinned on her white cape and apron. She completed her attire with a black head covering, the traditional Amish church outfit.

Elizabeth surveyed herself in the mirror making sure everything was securely pinned in place. She winced as a straight pin poked her. She wished they could be allowed to have snaps or buttons on their dresses, but those were considered worldly. Still, anything would be better than straight pins! Satisfied that everything was neatly in place she hurried down the stairs.

One hour later found Elizabeth seated in the Yoder's kitchen along with all the other girls her age. Women and girls sat in the kitchen on wooden benches that had been set up throughout the house, while the men and boys were seated in the living room. Amish church services lasted approximately three hours with each family taking a turn hosting the service in their home. Elizabeth felt guilty for sometimes wishing she could stay home from church. Sitting on the hard, backless benches so long made for a sore back. After the services were over, a light lunch was served. Because working on Sundays wasn't permitted, the traditional lunch was mixed peanut butter sandwiches (peanut butter mixed with corn syrup and marshmallow fluff to a spreading consistency), cheese, pickles, pickled beets, homemade bread, jam, coffee, and tea, with various cookies for desert.

At 9 A.M. sharp, everyone was seated and services began. Elizabeth listened as the hymn singing began. She soon found her mind wandering as she watched Ruby Mast, a young mother, with her three little girls. She is only twenty-one, thought Elizabeth. I don't want to get married until I'm at least twenty-three. She fought back the urge to giggle as she watched the three little girls. The two oldest each had a handkerchief that their mother had fashioned into dolls, in hopes of entertaining them during the long service. But instead of playing with the dolls, a contest of tug o' war began when the older girl tried to coerce the younger girl into trading with her. All the while a frustrated Ruby was trying to keep the toddler in her lap who had spotted her daddy in the next room.

It would sure be nice if families could sit together in church, thought Elizabeth. She watched as Ruby offered the girl a cracker to quiet her.

Her thoughts were interrupted when Bishop Joe arose and began to speak to the congregation. He began by thanking God for the opportunity to be together. Elizabeth listened as he read from the Bible: "Enter ye in at the straight gate for wide is the gate, and broad is the way that leads to destruction, and many there be which go in thereat. Because strait is the gate and narrow is the way, which leads into life, and few there be that find it" (Matthew 7:13,14).

Elizabeth felt a hollow feeling at the pit of her stomach as she heard the familiar words. Oh, if only one could ever know for certain that you were forgiven. She remembered with shame the times she'd cheated in a game or in her schoolwork. Afterwards she had felt sick with guilt but was too scared to admit it to anyone. Could God forgive her? She felt once again the guilt weighing down on her and tried to push the thoughts away.

Bishop Joe then went on to say that soon the world would end. Elizabeth felt a chill go up her spine. She knew the Amish teaching that when one was baptized, the sins of their past were washed away. But what about after that? she wondered. If only I could die the day I get baptized, then I could be certain that I'm going to heaven. But one had to be sixteen before being allowed to get baptized.

Then suddenly the thought hit her: What happened to people who died before they were baptized? Elizabeth shivered. She didn't want to think about that. She knew the

Amish frowned on people in other religions who said they knew they were saved and were sure of going to heaven. How can they know they are saved? she thought. Wouldn't one have to be perfect to be saved? Probably only martyrs who died for their faith knew for sure.

As much as Elizabeth wanted to know for sure, the thought of dying a martyr made a chill go up her spine. What was her faith? Was it their traditions, the way they dressed and their other customs?

Elizabeth tried to push the thoughts away and concentrate on the rest of the sermon.

Soon, to her relief, the last hymn was sung and the service was over.

Elizabeth stood up and stretched, glad to move around after sitting for three hours. Then she and Rachel went to help with lunch. The older ladies were hurrying to put the food on the makeshift tables that had been set up. They all talked and laughed as they ate, catching up on the latest community news.

Much later, when the last dish was washed and put away, Rachel asked Elizabeth, "Do you think we have time to take a walk before your dad is ready to go home?"

"I'll go ask."

Soon she was back, all smiles. "He says if we're back in one hour."

The girls hurried out the door and headed for the woods, their favorite spot. They could talk about anything here without being overheard by Rachel's little sisters.

"Can you believe we have only a few more weeks of school left in our lives?" Rachel said.

"Hardly," answered Elizabeth. "In some ways I wish it wasn't ending."

"I know I will be glad when we're done," Rachel spoke impatiently. "I can hardly wait to go with the youngie, can you?"

"Yes, I can wait." Elizabeth answered. "It's kinda scary to think of being all grown up."

"Well," smiled Rachel dreamily, "I want to have a beau and get married."

"Not me!" declared Elizabeth.

"Why not?"

"How will I know if he is the right one?" Elizabeth shook her head.

"If you love him, you'll know, I suppose," Rachel replied.

"Yes, but what about couples who date for a year or two then break up? What if they would've gotten married, then found out they were wrong for each other. Amish people can't get divorced."

"I guess you have a point," Rachel agreed.

"I think they probably get bored with each other," said Elizabeth.

"You mean, they lose the romantic feelings?"

"Exactly," nodded Elizabeth. "I think it would be nice to know someone cared for me but—"

"Do you think someone likes you?" Rachel interrupted.

"I didn't say that," said Elizabeth, her face getting red.

"Aha!" said Rachel. "You are blushing. I think you are keeping something from me."

Elizabeth hesitated, then confided, "The other night we were invited to Daniel and Anna for Daniel's birthday, and Anna's family was there too." She went on to tell Rachel how Matthew had winked at her at the supper table.

Rachel burst out laughing. "I wish I could've seen your face! Is he cute?"

"I suppose it depends on what you consider cute," Elizabeth shrugged.

Rachel laughed again. "I think someone finally got your attention."

"I still think it's bad manners to wink at a strange girl you don't even know."

"What did you do?"

"I stuck my nose in the air and just ignored him."

"You didn't!" Rachel was overcome by a fit of giggles as she pictured Elizabeth doing just that.

"I did!" Elizabeth stood up. "We'd better get back to the house," she said.

"Yes, I suppose," said Rachel, thinking to herself, We're not even out of school yet, and already life feels like its changing. She, for one, didn't mind the changes.

The last day of school finally arrived.

"Well, this is it," Rachel said as the two girls headed for the bus, diplomas in hand. "Our school days are finally over."

"Aren't you in the least bit sad?" Elizabeth asked. "It's like we're stepping into a whole new world. We won't get to see each other every day anymore."

"Yes, that makes me sad, but that's the only thing," said Rachel. "I know you would like to go on to high school and you feel like there's so much to learn yet, but not me. I'm glad for a good basic education."

"Yes, I know but I guess part of me would like time to stand still right where we're at," sighed Elizabeth.

"I think you are way too sentimental," laughed Rachel. "You are the only thing about school I will miss."

Chapter Three

June came, and with it Elizabeth's fifteenth birthday. Summer had officially begun. It was a busy time on the Hostetler farm—planting and weeding the garden, mowing the lawn, tending to the flowerbeds, and canning vegetables. Mother kept Elizabeth busy from dawn till dusk, and whenever she could spare her at home, she sent her to help the married children. This was a job Elizabeth looked forward to, spending time with her little nieces and nephews, reading them stories, holding the babies.

Elizabeth wished she weren't the youngest in her family. She wished her Mom would have a baby like Rachel's mom did last summer. It would be fun to have a little sister to play with.

"Mom, Rachel invited me to come for her birthday this Saturday and spend the night," said Elizabeth one day as they were weeding the garden.

"I'll ask Dad," said Mom. "If we get done with the thrashing I think we could spare you. You worked hard this summer. I think you deserve a treat."

"Oh, good!" Elizabeth felt like clapping her hands but she knew she was too old to show such emotion.

Finally Saturday arrived and the thrashing was finished. Elizabeth sighed with relief. It had been a long week. It was customary in the Amish community for all the neighbors to help each other with big jobs like thrashing wheat. The women would bake and cook all day to feed the hungry men. Elizabeth thought she'd never seen so much food or washed so many dishes in her life. But all that was forgotten, as she got ready to spend the night at Rachel's house.

"I thought today would never come," said Rachel as she came out to welcome Elizabeth.

"Same here," agreed Elizabeth. "I was afraid we wouldn't get done with all our work but thankfully we did or else I wouldn't be here."

"And am I ever glad," said Rachel. "Dad and Mom agreed to let us camp back by the creek tonight."

The two girls could hardly contain their excitement through the delicious supper of pizza and cake and ice cream made at Rachel's request. But soon supper was over and the girls were on their way to the creek, carrying their tent and sleeping bags.

"Well, what did you wish for when you blew out your candles?" asked Elizabeth, once the tent was set up.

"Hmm," sighed Rachel. "At this moment I feel like I have everything I could wish for. The only thing I'd change if I could is, I'd make this be my sixteenth birthday."

"My mom always says you shouldn't wish your life away," said Elizabeth.

"Yes, I know it's silly," said Rachel, "but Vern will be sixteen this year." Vern was a boy she had a crush on. "What if he finds a girlfriend before I'm sixteen?"

Elizabeth laughed. "You've got to be kidding! I would say then it wasn't meant to be." She said bluntly.

"But I can't imagine liking anyone else," sighed Rachel. "I've liked him ever since I was in third grade."

Elizabeth nodded. "I know and I think you're silly. We're too young to think of such things. Besides, if you are meant for each other, you will get together. Look at Linda and Nelson. They got back together again."

"I suppose you are right," agreed Rachel, as she laid down on her sleeping bag and yawned.

"Tired already?" asked Elizabeth.

"Yes," Rachel replied. "I've been really tired lately and I think I've lost some weight, too. My dresses hang on me, and now Mom has started me on some new vitamins."

"Are they helping?" asked Elizabeth.

"I can't tell a difference yet," Rachel yawned again. "I suppose it takes awhile, but Mom says I may have to go to the chiropractor for my headaches."

"Do you have them often?"

"More so lately, I guess," Rachel admitted.

The girls were silent for a while listening to the night sounds.

"My parents say this is the nicest time in our lives," said Elizabeth thoughtfully.

"Yes, my parents tell me that, too," said Rachel. "Do you really think that's true?"

"I don't know but I would like to stop time right now so we could go on this way forever." Elizabeth gazed up at the stars.

"As perfect as our lives seem right now, I suppose we would get tired of it," answered Rachel. "But then you know I think it's exciting when things change."

The two girls talked and giggled into the wee morning hours until they both fell asleep, dreaming of a bright and happy future.

Several weeks later a letter arrived for Elizabeth.

"There's a letter for you from Rachel," said Marilyn, handing Elizabeth an envelope.

"Oh good," said Elizabeth tearing it open.

I haven't seen her since I was there for her birthday, and she wasn't in church Sunday.

Dear Elizabeth,

I have been sick with the flu so Mom took me to the doctor. He says I need to come into the hospital for some tests on Friday. I hope I feel better soon. I just wanted to let you know.

Your best friend,

Rachel

"Anything wrong?" Mom asked, seeing Elizabeth's frown.

"Rachel's sick and has to go to the hospital for tests," Elizabeth answered, handing her mother the letter. "I hope it's nothing serious. Do you really think it could be?"

"Well, it doesn't sound good," Elizabeth's mother replied, "but let's not worry. It's all in God's hands."

Usually her mother's words reassured Elizabeth, but not today. She wished she could go over to see her best friend right now. Rachel must be so scared. Neither of them had ever been inside a hospital before. Surely it's nothing serious, she said to herself, trying to shake the feeling of heaviness. But Rachel was all she could think about that evening as she went about her chores.

It was a week later when Mom finally agreed that Elizabeth could hitch up old Charlie and drive over to the Yoder's to see Rachel. Elizabeth could hardly wait to get there. It was only four miles but it seemed to take forever.

It seemed strange to be going away by herself. She passed several Amish farms along the way. Everyone was busy with farm work or gardening. Elizabeth could hardly believe it was August already; summer would soon be over, but this year she wouldn't be going back to school—and she was glad, because this fall was special. They were busy getting ready for her older sister Linda's wedding. Nelson and Linda were getting married in November but, according to Amish tradition, it would be kept a secret until about three weeks before the big day.

Elizabeth fidgeted in her seat, wishing she could urge Charlie to go faster but she knew Dad wouldn't like her pushing the old horse too much in the warm August sun. Ah well, she sighed to herself, it's only one more mile.

Rachel spotted Elizabeth from her spot on the porch swing as she drove up to the hitching rack and hurried out to greet her.

"What brings you here?" she asked.

Elizabeth finished tying the horse and turned around to smile at her friend. "I just had to come see how you were. I heard you were in the hospital a few days?"

"Yes, I was," said Rachel, looking strange.

Elizabeth waited for her to say more as they walked back to the house, but Rachel kept silent.

Just as Elizabeth started to ask Rachel what was wrong, she glanced over and saw tears running down her cheeks. "Oh Rachel," she said worriedly, "Is it something bad?"

Rachel nodded, unable to speak. She reached over and took her friend's hand. It felt cold.

"The doctor said I have cancer," she said in a hoarse whisper.

Both girls were crying by now. Elizabeth wished she knew what to say. She wished it were a bad dream. She reached over and hugged Rachel, their tears mingling together.

How long they sat there like that Elizabeth didn't know; time seemed to stand still.

"Are they sure?" she finally asked.

Rachel nodded, wiping her tears with her handkerchief.

"Does it hurt?" asked Elizabeth.

Rachel shrugged. "Mostly I just feel tired."

"Where is the cancer?"

"It's in the blood," said Rachel. "I have leukemia."

"Maybe they are wrong!" cried Elizabeth. "Doctors make mistakes."

Rachel was quiet.

"What can they do?" Elizabeth asked amid tears, "Can they cure it?"

"I don't know," said Rachel her voice quivering. "They want to start chemo."

"When?' asked Elizabeth.

"Next week." Rachel stuffed her handkerchief back into her pocket..

"Then what?" asked Elizabeth.

"I don't know." Rachel shrugged. "I guess we'll have to see if it helps."

"It will," Elizabeth reassured her. "People are cured of cancer all the time."

"Will you come to the hospital to see me?" Rachel sounded scared.

"I'll come as often as I can," Elizabeth promised through her tears.

They hugged each other again as Elizabeth stood up to leave. "Remember all the plans we made and the things we talked about on the night of your birthday?"

"Yes," answered Rachel. "It was only three weeks ago, but it seems like so much longer. Do you think any of our dreams will come true?"

Elizabeth couldn't answer because of the big lump that welled up in her throat. Shrugging her shoulders, she hugged Rachel again.

"Why me?" Rachel cried.

Elizabeth shook her head. "I wish I knew," she answered. "What did your mom say?"

"Sometimes I see her wiping her tears and then I feel scared," Rachel whispered. "What if I ..." Rachel stopped. She couldn't say the word.

Elizabeth didn't want to hear any more. "I'd best get home," she said. "They will worry where I'm at."

"Thank you for coming," said Rachel.

Elizabeth drove home in a daze. She felt chilled all over and her head hurt from crying. How could this happen? Why did this happen? The questions kept going over and over in her mind. Two weeks ago life had seemed almost perfect.

"Where's Elizabeth?" asked Dad, as they sat down to eat their supper.

"She went over to see Rachel this afternoon," Mom replied. "She should be back by now though."

"Oh, you know how those two girls get to talking," said Marilyn. "They probably just lost track of time."

"Yah, I suppose you're right," said Mom, "but just the same I wish she were home."

"Here she is now." Leroy got up from the table, grabbed his hat, and hurried out to the barn. "I'll put the horse away for you," he offered. He took the horse by the bridle, then stopped when he saw her tears.

Elizabeth wiped furiously at her eyes, trying to swallow the lump in her throat. Following her brother into the barn, she sat down on a hay bale.

After feeding and watering the horse, Leroy came to join her. "What's wrong?" he asked again gently.

"It's Rachel," Elizabeth sobbed. "She has cancer."

"What?" Leroy looked stunned. "Are you sure?"

Elizabeth nodded. They sat in silence a few moments, then Leroy took her hand. "We'd better go in. They will wonder what's taking so long."

"I don't want any supper, she said. You go ahead."

"Sure you don't want me to stay?" he offered. "Mom made your favorite soup. It'll make you feel better."

Elizabeth stood to her feet. "Maybe you're right," she agreed.

Slowly they headed back to the house. "Isn't that a beautiful sunset," commented Leroy, hoping to lighten the mood.

"Yes it is," agreed Elizabeth stopping to admire it, but her mind was still on her friend. "What will happen if the chemo doesn't help Rachel?" she asked.

"I just don't know," Leroy replied. "But let's not even think like that."

"I suppose you're right," Elizabeth sighed. "But what if it were me?" Fear crept into her voice. "I'm not ready to die."

Leroy was taken aback by her words and was silent for several moments before answering. "I guess no one ever wants to die," he said at last.

"I mean, I don't think I'd go to heaven," Elizabeth sobbed.

"Oh Elizabeth, don't say that!" Leroy felt helpless, thinking about how often he too struggled with the same feeling. Who *was* good enough to go to heaven? They stood there for several moments watching the sun sink behind the hills, each lost in their own thoughts.

"Come on," Leroy said at last, breaking the silence. "Let's go in."

Chapter Four

"It sure is nice for October," said Mom as she and Elizabeth drove along the little winding country road to Daniel and Anna's farm.

"Is that why you chose October to get married?" asked Elizabeth.

"Yes, it was."

"How old were you when you got married?" Elizabeth was curious.

"I was only nineteen," said Mom. "Too young."

"How did you meet Dad?"

"I was just sixteen the first time I saw him. He came to work for his uncle Samuel who was our next-door neighbor. On Sunday evenings I would ride with him to the hymn singings."

Elizabeth wished she dared asked Mom how she knew Dad was the right one? But what would Mom think of her to ask such a question—and not even sixteen yet!

"Were you surprised when Dad asked you for a date?"

"Not really," Mom admitted. "We became friends that summer, then several weeks after he went home I received a letter from him asking for my friendship. Several days later I wrote back to say yes I would like that very much. Three months went by before I heard from him again. Everyday I would check the mail and no letter. I finally came to the conclusion that he'd changed his mind.

"One day I finally got my letter explaining what had happened," Mom continued her story. "When my letter to him arrived, his mother put it on his desk in his room. Somehow it slipped down behind the desk, and wasn't found until he moved his desk several months later."

"What happened then?" asked Elizabeth.

"Well, at first he didn't know what to do," Mom replied. "After all, three months had gone by already and he thought I may have changed my mind. But he decided to write and tell me what had happened and see if we could get together soon. To make a long story short, he came to see me soon after that and two years later we were married."

Elizabeth smiled, trying to picture her parents young and in love. She used to wonder if they were still in love as she had never seen them as much as hold hands, but if the smile on Mom's face was any indication of her feelings, Elizabeth thought she knew the answer to her question.

They drove in silence the rest of the way, one fondly reminiscing about the past, the other dreaming of a romantic future. The only sound breaking the silence was the rhythmic clip-clop of old Charlie's hooves.

When they arrived at Daniel's, Anna greeted them at the door holding baby Elaine.

"Come in, she smiled holding the screen door wide open. "My, am I ever glad to see you!

Elaine has been so fussy I haven't gotten anything done yet. Then, to top it all off, Bennie dumped the pail of milk Matthew brought in this morning, and when I rushed over to try to rescue him I slipped and fell in it!"

Elizabeth laughed at the funny sight it must've been. "What did you do?"

"Well, fortunately, Matthew came to my rescue. He took the baby while I went to change and then he took all three children out with him while I cleaned the mess. I was sure glad he was here as Daniel had just left for town. I don't know what I would've done if he hadn't been here."

"Well, it's sure nice to hear something good about myself, especially when I'm eavesdropping." Matthew came in through the back door.

"Oh Matthew." Anna smiled fondly at her younger brother. "You were a lifesaver this morning."

Excited barking from the dogs outside interrupted their conversation. "Oh no," Matthew groaned, seeing the cows in the yard. "I forgot to close the gate."

"Elizabeth," Mom ordered, "go help him."

The cows, with freedom in mind, had headed down the lane. For the next several minutes Matthew and Elizabeth chased them across the lawn and through the garden, finally cornering them between the barn and the corncrib.

"Can you keep them here while I take apart this makeshift gate?" called Matthew, running to get the pliers.

"I think so," said Elizabeth calling the dogs to help her stand guard.

After the cows were safely back in the barnyard, Matthew asked, "Can you hold this end of the gate while I fasten the other end?"

"I'll try," said Elizabeth. She held firmly to her end of the makeshift gate while Matthew tugged on the other end trying to get it in place. Just then the middle strand of barbed wire snapped, hitting Elizabeth's arm and cutting a long gash.

"Oh no, I'm sorry!" exclaimed Matthew when he saw what had happened. He quickly took her arm in both of his hands. "Here, let me see how bad it is," he said, inspecting the wound.

Elizabeth bit her lip to hold back the tears. "I'm okay," she said determined not to cry even though it was beginning to throb painfully.

Matthew hid a smile. Taking a clean handkerchief from his pocket, he gently wrapped it around her arm. His heart melted at the sight of her big brown eyes filled with tears, one rolling slowly down her cheek.

"I'm sorry, Elizabeth this is my fault." Matthew gently reached up and brushed away the tear with his thumb. "We'll see if your mom says it needs stitches."

"It's okay," Elizabeth said again.

Elizabeth's mother carefully cleaned the wound and bandaged it. "It should be all right now," she said. "You can take some aspirin if it starts to hurt. Now," she was back to business again, "it's almost lunchtime and we haven't gotten anything done yet. Elizabeth can watch the boys while we get it ready."

"I can help," Elizabeth insisted.

"Are you sure your arm is okay?" worried Anna.

"It's fine." She headed toward the kitchen, with both little boys following close behind.

Mom smiled as she heard Elizabeth talking to the boys. One thing to be said for Elizabeth, she thought, she has a lot of determination, even though that was the very thing that sometimes got her into trouble.

"This is very good chili," said Daniel, complimenting Anna at lunch.

"I'm afraid I can't take credit for it," said Anna. "Elizabeth made it."

"You know what they say, Elizabeth, the way to a man's heart, is through his stomach," teased Daniel. "This is good practice for you. You will soon be sixteen and can begin dating."

Elizabeth felt herself blush. "I'm not looking for a man to cook for," she protested.

Daniel laughed. "Still the same ol' Liz. Someday a guy will come along who will change your mind."

Elizabeth looked up ready to respond, but just then her eyes met Matthew's. His eyes twinkling mischievously, he winked at her.

Elizabeth glared at him, and she felt like kicking him under the table. How could he be so sweet one minute, and so irritating the next?

"I think I hear Elaine crying," said Anna, pushing her chair away from the table.

I'll get her," offered Elizabeth, hurrying toward the bedroom, glad for an excuse to escape the room.

"How's Elizabeth doing?" Daniel asked Mom after Elizabeth had left the room. "Is Rachel improving any?"

Mom hesitated before answering. "Elizabeth goes over to see her once a week or so. Doctors say it doesn't look good." She lowered her voice a bit. "But Elizabeth is trying to be so strong for Rachel's sake. I just don't know what'll happen to her if ... Well, you know how close those two girls have always been."

"May I go see Rachel tomorrow?" asked Elizabeth on their way home that afternoon.

"I'll have to ask Dad," Mom replied, "but I think it should be okay."

And so the next afternoon found Elizabeth on her way to the Yoder's house. It had been nearly two weeks since she had seen Rachel as she had just come home from the hospital two days earlier.

Mrs. Yoder met her at the door. "Come in," she welcomed her with a smile. "Rachel was hoping you'd come."

"How is she doing?" asked Elizabeth.

"She's weak and very tired," sighed Mrs. Yoder. "But you just go right on in. She'll be so glad to see you."

When Elizabeth entered Rachel's bedroom she caught her breath. The thin frail girl on the bed did not even look like her friend. Elizabeth felt a lump rise in her throat, her eyes stung with tears. As she moved closer to the bed, Rachel opened her eyes.

"Hi there," she said in a weak voice. "I didn't know anyone was here."

"Hi," said Elizabeth, trying to blink back her tears. "How are you feeling?"

"Tired," Rachel groaned. "Oh Elizabeth, it's awful!"

Elizabeth dropped to her knees beside the bed and took Rachel's hand. "Do you have to go again?"

Rachel nodded. "This is the worst part though," she sobbed, taking off her scarf.

"Oh, Rachel," was all Elizabeth could say. Almost all of Rachel's beautiful blonde hair was gone except for a few clumps.

Elizabeth hugged her, their tears mingling. "It's going to be okay," she reassured her. "It'll grow back. Who knows, maybe it'll grow in black like mine."

At this Rachel produced a wry smile. "I guess maybe I'm too vain. I know we aren't supposed to have pride in our appearance." She sighed. "Maybe I'm just wicked and God is punishing me for liking my blonde hair too much."

"I don't think so," said Elizabeth. God gave you blonde hair."

"I know, but I don't want anyone to see me this way," sobbed Rachel.

"I understand," said Elizabeth sympathetically. "But just think. If this is the price you have to pay to get well, it will be worth it, won't it?"

"Well, *if* it helps." Rachel put the emphasis on the word *if*. "But what if I don't get better?" Her voice was filled with fear.

"Don't say that!" said Elizabeth, hating to hear Rachel talk about the very thing she tried not to think about every night before she fell asleep. Rachel had to get better! Fifteen-year-old girls weren't supposed to die. "Don't even think it!"

"I do think about it though," Rachel replied, her voice barely a whisper. "What if I die? I just don't know if I'd go to heaven." Her voice trailed off.

"I feel the same way," agreed Elizabeth. "I know we pray before every meal, and when we get up in the mornings and Dad prays, and at night before we go to bed. We go to church, but . . ." She paused, trying to find the right words. "Jesus doesn't feel real to me. I mean I know the Bible is true but I wish I knew if—"

"If you are saved?" asked Rachel. "I know what you mean," she went on. "Before I got sick I thought I would have a pretty good chance of going to heaven because, well, we are Amish. I've always tried to obey all the church rules so why do I feel so lost? Maybe if I read my Bible more, I'll feel better."

Elizabeth nodded her head in agreement, then, wanting to change the subject to a lighter note, she said, "Speaking of reading, I brought a book over. I thought maybe I could read a couple chapters to you every time I come over."

Rachel smiled. "What book is it?" she asked.

Elizabeth grinned. "My favorite. Gold Alaska."

Rachel laughed. "What else could it be? If I know you, you probably wish you could've been part of that whole wagon train going west in search of gold."

Elizabeth smiled but didn't answer. She just began reading and, for the next hour, Rachel momentarily forgot her pain as Elizabeth read page after page, stopping now and then to comment and laugh.

"Maybe someday I'll get to travel west," she sighed dreamily when she put the book down. "But I suppose for now I'd best get home."

"Thank you for coming," said Rachel sleepily. Her eyes falling shut before Elizabeth slipped out the door.

"Steven will bring the horse around for you," said Mrs. Yoder. She also thanked Elizabeth for coming.

Steven echoed his mother's thanks when he brought the horse up to the edge of the walks.

"We're always glad when you come to see Rachel."

"I'm glad I can help," said Elizabeth sincerely. "I'd best get going," she gave a good-bye wave.

Poor Steven, she thought, riding away. He was Rachel's oldest brother and at seventeen he was tall and gangly and terribly shy. Elizabeth smiled as she thought back to their school days, remembering how nervous he was, especially with girls around. She could sympathize with his habit of blushing. She felt her cheeks burn again at the memory of Daniel's teasing yesterday—in front of Matthew, of all people! Steven hadn't made her blush today, she realized. "Oh well, I know him better," she said to herself, urging Charlie to hurry up. There were chores waiting to be done.

Chapter Five

The next few weeks passed by all too quickly with everything that had to be done before the wedding. The Hostetler's farm was scrubbed from top to bottom, with nearby relatives helping with the preparations. There was sewing to be done also, including the traditional blue dress with the white organdy cape and apron for the bride. Then there were long tables to be set up, enough to seat at least two hundred guests. The bridal table in the corner of the living room received the most attention. It was decorated in the bride's favorite color and with all the best china.

Aunts and neighbor ladies were chosen to prepare the two big meals for the day-long affair, and friends from the youth group would serve.

"My, I sure didn't remember that getting ready for a wedding was this stressful!" said Linda, the day before the wedding. She took a moment to sit down and catch her breath.

"I wish it were over already."

"You just need to calm down and take a break," said Marilyn.

"Who needs a break?" asked Dena, who had come down to the basement to begin decorating the cake.

"Me," said Linda. "I feel so stressed out. I just said to Marilyn I wish it were over already."

Just then a voice called from upstairs. "Linda, you're needed up here."

"Here we go again," sighed Linda, heading for the stairs.

"Is there anything I can help with?" asked Marilyn setting the bowl of frosting on the table.

"I don't think so," said Dena, tying on an apron. "I left Elizabeth with all the children though; she could probably use a hand." She stopped her stirring, then commented, "I can't believe that in a few months she will be sixteen."

"Yes, and she would have everyone believe there's not a guy out there that she would give a second glance," said Marilyn.

Dena laughed. "She *is* very independent. But how about you? Who is your partner for the wedding?"

"Nelson's cousin from out of state. I've never met him."

"Well, you know what they say about weddings," warned Dena laughingly. "They always make new couples." She paused, then continued. "I don't think enough of our young people take finding a life partner seriously. Does it bother you, Marilyn, that you are already almost nineteen and no beau?"

"Yes and no," Marilyn replied. "When all my friends are with their special friends I wish I had someone too, but after the heartache from my last experience, I know I'm not ready to date casually. This time I want to pray about it first."

"Wise choice," Dena agreed.

The big day finally arrived. The Hostetler's home was abuzz with activity as the ladies arrived who had been chosen to prepare the food to be served that day. As was tradition, the three-hour wedding ceremony was already in progress at the nearest Amish neighbor's home, giving time for the food to be prepared for the reception to be held in the bride's home immediately following the ceremony.

Elizabeth took special pains getting dressed in her new light blue dress and matching cape and apron, made especially for the occasion. Hair preparation came next. With a twinge of guilt, she daringly combed it straight back, omitting the usual part in the center that the rules required. She knew she really shouldn't, but today was special. It was her first time to ever have a part in a wedding. Maybe Mom would be too busy to notice, she thought, pulling out a few curly little bangs—the ones Mom was always telling her to tuck under her covering.

Taking one last look in the mirror, making sure everything was just as she wanted it, she got out her forbidden hair spray to hold the locks in place. Then she hurried downstairs to greet Nancy, her serving partner.

Nancy had a friendly outgoing personality and Elizabeth knew immediately that she would enjoy working with her. She studied her appearance as they worked. She liked the way Nancy combed her dark auburn hair loosely on her forehead, and her dress fit absolutely perfect, like a glove. Elizabeth knew Mom would never let her wear her dress that short.

Their dresses were supposed to be eight inches off the floor, and Nancy's had to be at least twelve inches. But she knew that Nancy's community was more liberal. Even the shiny, silky material of Nancy's dress wouldn't be acceptable in Elizabeth's community. She wished she dared to have such a fancy dress.

"What shall we do now?" asked Nancy, interrupting her thoughts.

"I guess we could start slicing the cheese," said Elizabeth. "That's at the top of the list."

The two girls began to get acquainted as they worked in one corner of the basement.

"I'm looking forward to having Nelson and Linda as our next door neighbors," said Nancy.

"Maybe you and I will get to see each other oftener that way."

"Yes, that would be nice," Elizabeth agreed, thinking it would be nice to have Nancy for a friend.

Just then several older teenage boys interrupted them.

"Need someone to show you how it's done?" asked one of the boys, smiling flirtatiously at Nancy.

Nancy smiled back. "Are you sure you know how?" she asked.

Elizabeth felt nervous and tongue-tied. She wanted to escape without notice before someone said something to her to make her blush.

But Nancy didn't seem to mind. She went on laughing and talking several more minutes before coming over to help make the date pudding.

"Do you know those guys?" asked Elizabeth, surprised that any girl not yet sixteen could talk so easily with the "youngie" boys.

"Yes, I know Eugene." Nancy nodded toward the taller boy who had spoken to her first.

"He's from our community. But I don't know who the other two are."

Elizabeth admired the way Nancy seemed so at ease around boys. "Guys make me nervous," she blurted out. Nancy looked surprised. "They are just guys, what's there to be nervous about? They like to tease girls and they like it when we talk back. Don't you like it?"

Elizabeth shrugged. "I try to avoid them."

"When will you be sixteen?" asked Nancy.

"In June," answered Elizabeth. "When is your birthday?"

"In January."

"Will you start dating right away?" asked Elizabeth. A girl like Nancy would have no problem getting a date.

"If the right one asks me." Nancy smiled.

"And who is the right one?" asked Elizabeth curiously.

Nancy glanced around, making sure no one else was close by. "That one," she whispered, motioning toward the guy she'd referred to as Eugene earlier.

Elizabeth smiled. He certainly looked like Nancy's type. Not a hair out of place from his short layered haircut down to his cowboy boots.

"The one with the fancy haircut?" asked Elizabeth.

"Yes, isn't he cute?" giggled Nancy.

"I guess so," answered Elizabeth. "But doesn't he get in trouble for having such a fancy haircut? No one would ever get away with that in our community—or with wearing cowboy boots. That would be simply unheard of!"

"Well, they are not really allowed for us in our community either," said Nancy. "But most of the young boys in our community do things like that before they become members of the church."

"Is it true that the 'youngie' get together and have wild parties on Saturday evenings?" asked Elizabeth. She had heard some of the older people in her church talk about the wild "going-ons" with the "youngie" in that community.

Nancy laughed. "Yes, but my mom says they are just sowing their wild oats. They will settle down when they are ready to get married."

Elizabeth had heard that before too, but she doubted very much whether her parents would agree with that.

At last all the food was prepared. Everyone then made their way next door to where the ceremony was already in progress.

Elizabeth felt a lump in her throat as she watched Linda and Nelson stand before the minister answering yes to the questions that would unite them in marriage. She knew she was being sentimental but she wished that their family could stay just the same always, and that nothing would ever change.

When the ceremony was over, everyone hurried back to the house to start setting steaming bowls of food on the table. Nothing was left out. There was fried chicken, mashed potatoes, gravy, mixed vegetables, coleslaw, homemade bread, butter, jam, and cheese.

And for dessert there were three different kinds of pie, angel food cakes, fruit salad and date pudding. The next two hours were spent serving food to the over two hundred guests.

"I am sick of looking at food!" moaned Nancy later that afternoon, once they had a free moment to escape to Elizabeth's room.

"Me too," agreed Elizabeth, "but we still have to serve supper yet."

"It sounds like they are washing dishes now," said Nancy. "Do we have to help?"

"I don't think we'll be missed if we stay here a little longer," said Elizabeth. "Unless," she added mischievously, "you want to go see if they need help at Eugene's table?"

Nancy laughed at Elizabeth's teasing. "That's a thought but I'll opt for taking a break. But you haven't told me yet if there's someone you'd like to help?"

Elizabeth shrugged. "No, I didn't see anyone."

"Aw, come on," coaxed Nancy. "I told you. Surely there is someone you like even just a teeny."

Elizabeth felt funny talking this way to anyone besides Rachel. In fact, she couldn't remember ever admitting to anyone even liking a boy. "I, well ..." She felt embarrassed to go on. "I don't really like him.. I hardly know him. I uh…I just think he's kinda cute."

"Who?" asked Nancy. "Do I know him?"

Elizabeth nodded. "Matthew Yoder." There she'd said it!

Nancy gasped. "Matthew Yoder from our community? I'll say he's cute! How do you know him?"

"His sister Anna is married to my brother," Elizabeth answered.

"Get in line," Nancy laughed. "All the girls like Matthew."

"He doesn't even know I exist. Besides," Elizabeth felt silly. She wanted to change the subject. "Besides," she repeated, "we'd best go help with the dishes."

Nancy laughed. "Ah so we've uncovered a touchy subject."

"No we haven't," protested Elizabeth, "because I refuse to discuss it any further."

"In that case we may as well go help with the dishes," grinned Nancy, heading for the door.

The rest of the afternoon passed quickly. First there was the traditional hymn singing by the men folks, and then the bride and groom opened their gifts. Elizabeth and Nancy were kept busy washing dishes, resetting tables and preparing for the evening meal. First the older couples and young children were served. Then the tables were set again for the "youngie," this time with candles, fancy desserts, candy dishes, and punch, and each guy choosing a girl to sit by his side. Afterward they would sing hymns chosen by the bride and groom. All too soon the long-awaited day was over.

Elizabeth's feet ached as she climbed the stairs to her room. What a wonderful day it has been, she thought as she climbed into bed. Linda had never looked prettier. She and Nelson made the perfect couple. Everything about the day had been special, she thought.

She made friends with Nancy and even Matthew came for the affair. She smiled to herself in the dark thinking about the little smile he'd given her. "You're being silly," she said to herself. "You are only fifteen and too young to even think about boys." With that in mind, she rolled over and fell asleep.

Chapter Six

Now that the excitement of the wedding was over, life went back to normal.

This was Elizabeth's first winter home from school and her mother was going to teach her to sew her own coat and more complicated things. Elizabeth knew that most Amish girls could sew all their own clothes by the time they were sixteen.

"Mom," she asked one forenoon while they were sitting at the sewing machine, "do you suppose I could make Rachel a nightgown for Christmas?"

"I think that would be nice," said Mom. "She does spend a lot of time in bed, doesn't she?"

"Yes, she does," answered Elizabeth. "Oh Mom, sometimes I wonder if she'll ever get better. Do you think she will?"

"I just don't know," answered Mom.

"Mom," Elizabeth started hesitantly, "what if ... if, uh, Rachel would die before she gets baptized?"

"Well I don't know," answered Mom slowly. "God is a fair and just God."

"Would the ministers consider bending the rules to baptize her even though she's not sixteen?"

"I really don't know that a situation like this has come up before," said Mom, "but I'm sure they would bring it before the church so the members could vote on it."

"You mean someone might object?" Elizabeth couldn't believe that.

"I'm sure some of the people would have concerns about it," Mom replied.

"About baptizing someone who is probably dying?" asked Elizabeth in disbelief.

"Certainly," said Mom. "You know our people don't take making changes lightly or allowing anything new."

Elizabeth felt frustrated. It didn't make sense! she thought to herself. Didn't the Bible say to be baptized? "Some of our church rules don't make sense to me," she finally muttered.

"Now Elizabeth!" Mom rebuked her sharply. "I don't want to hear you say such things.

This way of life was good enough for our forefathers and it's good enough for us.

Besides," she continued, "it's not our job to understand all the rules, just to obey them."

Elizabeth kept silent. She knew it wouldn't do any good to say any more on the subject.

Mom was a stickler to keep every letter of the law.

"May I go see Rachel tomorrow?" asked Elizabeth that afternoon as she worked on sewing her friend's nightgown.

"Not tomorrow," said Mom. "Anna, Dena and Linda are coming over to bake the Christmas cookies and make the candy."

"Oh good," said Elizabeth. "I'm glad this year I'll get to be home for all the fun stuff."

The next day was every bit as good as Elizabeth had hoped. There were dozens of cookies, caramel and chocolate candy, and homemade taffy, and there were babies to hold.

Elizabeth wished the day would never end. She loved the special feeling of getting ready for Christmas. Making and hiding Christmas presents. Trying to guess what she would get.

"I don't think I ever ate so much candy in one day," she laughed as she helped Marilyn clean up the kitchen that evening after supper.

"I know what you mean," Marilyn agreed. But you never gain an ounce," she said enviously.

Just then a knock at the door interrupted their conversation.

"I wonder who that could be?" said Mom, laying her mending aside. "Why, hello, Mrs. Clayton," she greeted their next-door neighbor. "Come on in out of the cold."

"Yes, it has been a cold winter," said Mrs. Clayton conversationally.

"Won't you sit down for a cup of tea?" Mom asked.

"Oh, I'd really love to, but I came to ask a favor. Tom's uncle who lives out of town died, and we'd like to go to the funeral, but Jill and Nicole are afraid to stay alone so we were wondering if Elizabeth could come spend the night with her. It'd only be for one night," she added.

"Let me go check with my husband," said Mom, "but I think that'd be okay."

In a few minutes she returned. "Yes, that'd be fine," she said. "And if there's anything else we can do, let us know. And give Tom our sympathies." she added opening the door for Mrs. Clayton.

"Oh, thank you so much," said Mrs. Clayton. "We were truly been blessed to have such good people like you for neighbors."

"It works both ways," said Mom. "You were always there when we needed a favor too."

Elizabeth hurriedly finished her chores the next afternoon to be ready when the Claytons picked her up.

"All ready to go?" asked Mom, as Elizabeth came down carrying her overnight bag.

"Yes, I think so," said Elizabeth.

"Now you behave," said Mom sternly. "Jill and Nicole live a completely different lifestyle than how you were raised. You know how we Amish believe and what our rules are."

"Yes, I know," said Elizabeth. "Mrs. Clayton is here now. I'll be home tomorrow."

"Hi," said Jill, meeting Elizabeth at the door.

"Hi," Elizabeth smiled back.

"There's a pizza in the oven for your supper," said Mrs. Clayton. "And there are chips in the pantry for a snack." She went on, giving Jill last-minute instructions.

"Are you ready to go?" asked Mr. Clayton, coming in the back door. "I've got the car all packed."

"Yes, I believe that's it," said Mrs. Clayton. "I sure hope I didn't forget anything."

"Where's Nicole?"

"I'm right here, Dad," said Nicole. "I wish I could go with you."

"I don't think you'd like it," said Mr. Clayton. Sitting down beside the table he pulled her into his lap. You are eight years old now so you have to be a big girl. You will have more fun here with Jill. And we will be back tomorrow evening," he promised. "Daddy will pray with you before we leave."

"Ok," she agreed, giving him a big hug.

Everyone gathered in a circle and Elizabeth listened as Mr. Clayton prayed.

"Dear heavenly Father," he began, "we thank you for this day. We thank you for sending us your Son Jesus. We ask that you would be with the girls while we are gone and protect them and keep them safe. We ask that you would be with us too, Lord, and keep us safe as we travel. Bless Elizabeth for helping us."

Elizabeth listened as he prayed. She had never heard anyone pray like this before. At home they prayed from a prayer book, never their own words. She liked the way he had even asked God to bless her. She wished her family prayed like this. But she was sure her parents would not approve of this.

After Mr. Clayton ended the prayer, he and his wife hugged and kissed both girls, and in a flurry of last minute instructions they were gone.

Elizabeth could never imagine having Dad give her a kiss. Their family never showed such emotions. She looked around the kitchen as Jill got the pizza out of the oven. She liked the cozy little room. Everything was decorated in blue. Even their phone was blue. She tried to imagine what it would be like to have a phone. She could call Rachel anytime she wanted, but it was no use to wish for such things.

Amish people didn't allow phones in their homes. If they wanted to use the phone, they went to their neighbor's or to town.

Sometimes Elizabeth felt guilty for always wishing for things that were against the rules.

"What shall we do now?" Jill asked her after supper. "Would you like to watch a movie?"

"Sure," Elizabeth smiled. She could count the times on one hand that she'd seen a movie.

"We got a movie about pioneers going west," Jill grinned. "I know how much you like those kind of books." she added.

Elizabeth smiled. Westerns were her favorite. And so for the next two hours she sat, her eyes glued to the television screen.

Jill smiled as she watched Elizabeth's face. She couldn't imagine growing up without TV and electricity. "What shall we do now?" she asked, once the movie was over.

"I'd love to play computer games," Elizabeth replied.

"Why don't you go ahead and pick a game while I tuck Nicole in bed?" said Jill

Much later, and well past Elizabeth's usual bedtime, the two girls climbed the stairs to Jill's room.

"I don't know about you but I'm not tired yet," said Jill. "Are you?" "Not really," said Elizabeth. She felt strange being away from home for the night.

"I know what," Jill giggled. "Let's exchange clothes. I've always wanted to put on your little bonnet," referring to Elizabeth's head covering.

Elizabeth hesitated. "Are you sure you want to try on my clothes?" she asked, surprised.

"Yes," declared Jill. "Let's do it. I'll put on your clothes and you put on a pair of my jeans."

She pulled a pair out of her dresser drawer. "And you can pick out a sweater from my closet."

Elizabeth hesitated for a second. What would her mom say if she knew? But it's just for fun, she thought, selecting a pink sweater with flowers. "I like pink and I've never worn anything with flowers," she said.

Putting it on, she admired herself in the mirror. She felt strange. Her hair came down past her waist, and her legs looked long in jeans.

"You look great," said Jill. "Can I put makeup on you?"

"I guess so," agreed Elizabeth. "It's just for fun," she added.

"Do you ever wish you could wear makeup?" asked Jill, as she brushed some blush across Elizabeth's cheeks.

"I don't know," said Elizabeth. "I've never worn any before, and no one else in our family does either because we aren't allowed to."

"Does it bother you to be different?" asked Jill curiously.

"According to us you are the one that's different," she laughed, pointing at Jill in her Amish clothes.

At this both girls burst into a fit of giggles.

After much parading in front of the mirror in their strange clothes and more giggling, Jill and Elizabeth donned nightgowns and nestled down in bed.

"This was fun, wasn't it," said Jill sleepily.

"Yes," Elizabeth replied, smiling in the dark.

"I guess we aren't so different after all, are we?" .

"I guess not," agreed Elizabeth and with that both girls drifted off to sleep.

"Oh Elizabeth, this is so nice," said Rachel, admiring the new nightgown that Elizabeth had brought her. "I can use this next week when I go back to the hospital for more chemo treatments."

"I didn't know you were going again," said Elizabeth, a sinking feeling at the pit of her stomach.

"I just found out today," sighed Rachel.

"You've got to keep fighting this," encouraged Elizabeth. "You can beat this, you have to."

"I hope so. I'm sick of being sick."

The girls sat in silence, each lost in their own thoughts.

Elizabeth wished she could think of something to say to lighten the mood and cheer up her friend.

"I spent the night at Jill's last night," Elizabeth said. "I wish you could've been there." She proceeded to tell Rachel all about her evening of excitement.

"Did you really try on jeans?" asked Rachel, smiling at the thought, forgetting her own problems for the moment.

Elizabeth nodded. "I've already wished for some when I help with the haying," she admitted. "But putting on lipstick was the most fun. I've always wanted to do that."

"Your mom would faint if she knew you done that!" exclaimed Rachel, knowing how strict Mrs. Hostetler was.

"It was just for fun," defended Elizabeth.

"Would you ever consider leaving the Amish?" asked Rachel.

"Whatever makes you ask something like that?" Elizabeth was shocked at the question.

"Oh, I don't know, said Rachel." It's just that, well, you always say you wish you could get a high school education, and now you even tried on 'English' clothes." She paused, waiting for Elizabeth to answer.

Elizabeth laughed, "I know I'm different, but I don't think I'll leave just yet."

"I talk about getting married and you talk about traveling to Alaska or some such place and going to high school," said Rachel.

Elizabeth shrugged." I guess maybe I dream too much."

"What about getting married?" asked Rachel. "Isn't that every girl's dream?"

"I just can't picture myself getting married."

"Not even to Matthew?" teased Rachel.

Elizabeth shook her head. "He doesn't even know I exist."

Both girls fell silent again.

"Have you been reading your Bible like we talked about?" asked Rachel, breaking the silence.

Elizabeth shook her head, "Oh Rachel, I feel so guilty about it. I tried, but it seemed there were always so many distractions with getting ready for Linda's wedding and all, that I just got sidetracked. When I try to read," she confessed, "my mind keeps wandering, and I just don't understand it very well."

Rachel nodded understandingly." I've been reading more lately," she said, "and the more I read, the more I'm beginning to understand. I know there has to be answers in there for our questions, about knowing whether or not you are going to heaven."

"There must be," Elizabeth agreed. "I'm going to try and read it more. I have to find the answers somewhere." She gave her friend a hug before leaving.

Chapter Seven

To Elizabeth it seemed as though Christmas was over almost before it began.

"Don't you wish Christmas came oftener?" she asked Marilyn as they were working on the week's ironing.

"No, I don't," said Marilyn," I think I've gained ten pounds. It's not fair that you can eat so much and never gain an ounce!"

"It's all the hard work I do," Elizabeth joked. "Like ironing with these old flat irons. I wish we could have the ones that run off gas like some Amish churches do," she said.

"The Bible says to be content with what you have," Marilyn admonished her.

Elizabeth didn't answer. It just didn't make sense; they were allowed to have motors that ran on gas but not irons. Elizabeth knew it wouldn't do to share her opinion with Marilyn.

"Did you make any New Year's resolutions?" asked Marilyn, changing the subject.

"Not really," answered Elizabeth, "but I would like to read more books, and maybe start keeping a diary. And," she added, "I want to try and read my Bible everyday. How about you?" she asked her sister.

"Lose ten pounds is on the top of my list," laughed Marilyn.

Elizabeth laughed too. She wished she and Marilyn would always get along this way. But usually Marilyn was very reserved, unlike Elizabeth. I wish I were more quiet like Marilyn, she thought. Maybe I wouldn't get into so many disagreements with Mom over the rules. Yes, she decided, another resolution was in order: Learn to keep quiet.

"Did anyone bring the mail in yet?" asked Dad, as he washed his hands before lunch.

"Not yet," answered Mom, placing a steaming hot casserole in the center of the table.

"I'll go," offered Leroy, slipping into his boots. "Maybe my hunting magazine came today."

"I wish I would get a magazine," said Elizabeth as she sliced the homemade bread.

"You read too much as it is," her mom said.

Elizabeth opened her mouth to protest but then thought better of it. Dad wouldn't allow her disagreeing with Mom.

"We got a letter from Grandma," Leroy announced, handing Mom the mail.

"Aren't you going to read it?" asked Elizabeth.

"It can wait," said Mom." Lunch is on the table."

"Ah, go ahead," Dad smiled. "The food will stay warm a few minutes longer. He knew how much his wife enjoyed hearing from her aged parents.

Mom smiled at her husband as she opened her letter. She wished that her parents lived closer but they preferred the warmer climate of Florida, especially during the winter.

"Oh no," exclaimed Mom, looking up from her letter. "Dad broke his hip. Mom is wondering if we could come help her take care of him for a couple of weeks."

Dad was deep in thought, then he said, "I don't see why not. This isn't a busy time for us."

"But I don't think we can be gone for two weeks," Mom fretted. "There's butchering to be done."

"We can do that when we get back," Dad reassured her.

In the end Mom was persuaded that everything would be fine without them, and so for the next two days Elizabeth was kept busy helping her parents get clothes ready for the trip.

"Elizabeth, I've made a list of all I want you to do while we are gone," her mother told her the day they were to leave. "Especially, don't forget to help Daniel and Anna butcher on Thursday."

"I know, it's on the list" said Elizabeth. "Don't worry, I'll get everything done."

Finally, with many last minute instructions, they were off.

Elizabeth watched by the window until they were out of sight. It felt strange to be alone. She looked at the clock. It was 1:15; she had the whole afternoon ahead of her. Might as well get started on her jobs now, she thought, as she got out her mother's to-do list. Mending was her least favorite job. Maybe it would be better to get that out of the way first.

Elizabeth hummed as she worked. "Maybe if I hurry I can make my favorite chocolate chip cookies," she said to herself. "I could make some to take along to Daniel and Anna's tomorrow."

Elizabeth finished the mending in record time, leaving the afternoon to drag on endlessly. The house is too quiet, she thought. Maybe that is how Grandma Hostetler feels, thinking of her 89-year-old grandma who lived alone. Maybe I should take her some cookies too. Grandma Hostetler lived in a little house on uncle Levi's farm. It was tradition among the Amish for the youngest son to inherit the farm and then, in return, he built a small house close by or attached to the original farmhouse for his parents to live in for the remainder of their years.

Elizabeth liked visiting her grandma. She was very old fashioned; all her walls were painted white with only one braided rug by the door. Each time they went to visit her, she served molasses cookies and iced tea. Elizabeth thought they tasted better than anyone else's. She knew Grandma was very strict about keeping all the rules, She still did everything the way her mother had taught her. Elizabeth thought that Mom was too strict, but at least she allowed her to wear light colors, even though Grandma didn't think they should.

Elizabeth got out the sugar and eggs and the rest of the ingredients. At last the big bowl of cookie dough was ready to bake. Elizabeth hurried to put the cookies in the oven to bake, then sat down to read, sighing contentedly, as she curled up on the couch. This was great, she thought, reading in the middle of the afternoon. Maybe it wouldn't be so bad having Mom gone, after all.

Elizabeth was soon lost in her book, reading page after page. Suddenly, she was brought back to reality by the putrid smell of burning cookies.

"Oh no!" she cried, grabbing a pair of potholders and removing the charred pan. A thick haze of blue smoke filled the kitchen. Elizabeth hurriedly opened the window and, taking the burnt cookies outside, she threw them in the garbage, hoping to get rid of the evidence. She knew she would get a scolding if Marilyn found out.

Determined not to let the second batch burn, Elizabeth stayed in the kitchen and scrubbed the black pans while keeping an eye on the oven.

"It sure seems strange around here without Mom and Dad," said Leroy, as they sat down to eat supper.

"Yes, it does," agreed Elizabeth. "The house was so quiet this afternoon, it made me think we should visit Grandma more often."

Leroy nodded in agreement.

"Are you going to go help with the butchering at Daniel and Anna's tomorrow?" asked Elizabeth.

"Yes. I'm leaving at 7:30 so you had better be ready," he warned.

"I will, said Elizabeth. "Don't worry."

Elizabeth hurried to help with the chores the next morning, then rushed in to fix breakfast while Marilyn got ready to teach school. It's sure easier when Mom's home," she thought.

"Better bring the big buggy robe," warned Leroy. "It's two below zero, and your feet will be frozen by the time we get there."

Leroy was right. Elizabeth's feet felt like ice cubes by the time they got to Daniel's house.

"Come in," called Anna, holding the door open. "I have a cup of hot chocolate waiting for you. You're probably half frozen. I told Daniel this morning I think we picked the coldest day in February to butcher."

"My feet are cold, but otherwise I'm fine," Elizabeth accepted the steaming cup gratefully..

"Well, I'm glad you and Leroy could both make it," Anna rambled on. "My folks couldn't make it today so they sent Lamar and Matthew."

Matthew! Elizabeth didn't hear anything else Anna said. She never gave it a thought that HE might be here.

"So I thought maybe you could help them cutting up the meat in the basement," Anna went on. "As soon as you warm up a bit, I'll take you down to get started."

"Oh, I'm warmed up," said Elizabeth, tying on her apron. "I'll just go wash my hands before I get started."

Elizabeth shut the door of the washroom and checked her appearance in the small mirror. After washing her hands, she adjusted her head covering and pulled out a few little bangs. She wanted to look her best today.

Back in the living room, she saw Anna open the door and admit the two boys. "I brought you a helper," she was saying to them, "So don't be teasing her."

Both boys smiled at her.

"We won't chase her away," Lamar promised, "as long as she helps us."

Elizabeth tried to concentrate as Anna instructed her on what there was to be done.

"Trim off all the fat and put it in these buckets," she was saying. "Mom said she will come in a few days to help me make the soap from the animal fat. And put the steaks in this bucket as you cut them," she finished.

"You can help me at this table," Lamar invited.

"Aw, come on," Matthew protested. "That's not fair. You always get all the pretty girls."

Elizabeth felt her face get red.

"Now see what you went and did?" Lamar chided. "You made her blush."

Anna laughed. "That's enough guys," she said as she headed for the stairs.

Elizabeth almost wished she could follow Anna but she was soon at ease as the conversation turned to other things.

"Let me know when you are done cutting up the steaks, Elizabeth," Matthew said, "and I'll carry them up to Anna for you. The bucket gets pretty heavy."

Elizabeth nodded and smiled her thanks, wishing she could think of something to say. She knew Matthew was trying to be nice to make up for teasing her earlier.

Matthew looked over at Elizabeth as she worked; she certainly was cute with those big brown eyes and that sweet shy smile of hers. I'll have to see if I can get her to come and help me at my table, he thought.

The rest of the morning passed quickly as the three of them were kept busy cutting up the meat that Daniel and Leroy kept bringing in.

"Elizabeth," Anna finally called from the top of the stairs, "could you come help me finish lunch?"

"Be right up." Then, looking at Matthew, she asked, "Would you finish cutting these pork steaks for me?"

"Be happy to."

"How'd she end up helping you?" Lamar asked.

Matthew shrugged. "She took pity on me, I guess."

Lamar laughed, "It had nothing to do with her being cute, huh ?"

Just then Daniel and Leroy came in and, much to Matthew's relief, the subject was dropped.

"I'll wash the dishes and clean up the kitchen for you if you want to go help with the butchering," Elizabeth said to Anna when they finished with lunch. "It'll give you a break. I'll even put the kids down for their nap."

"I can't turn that down." Anna smiled her thanks at Elizabeth. "It's been a long time since I got to spend an afternoon with my little brothers."

Anna was glad for the opportunity to visit with her brothers while they worked, getting caught up on all the latest news from her home community.

"Well Lamar, can we expect wedding bells to be ringing for you and Rosemary?" she asked.

Lamar was quiet a moment. "We're talking about it," he finally admitted.

"How about you, Matthew?" Anna pried.

"What about me?" asked Matthew innocently.

"Are you ready to settle down and get serious about a girl?" Anna asked bluntly.

"Aw, come on," he laughed. "I'm too young for that."

"Well, if you're so young," said Anna, "then run upstairs and get a couple buckets out of the pantry for me."

Happy to escape from the conversation, Matthew gladly obliged.

"Now where could they be?" he muttered as his eyes scanned the shelves in the dimly lit pantry.

Just then Elizabeth came in carrying the leftover cake from lunch and placing it on the shelf. "What are you looking for?"

"Anna sent me after some more buckets, but I can't seem to find them," he answered.

"Here they are," said Elizabeth, bending down to pick them up.

Matthew had spotted them and bent to retrieve them at the same time. Thud! Their heads bumped together.

Elizabeth tried to step aside only to bump into him again.

"Sorry," she said, feeling breathless at his nearness. Her heart pounded faster when he stepped even closer until his body was lightly touching against hers.

Matthew placed his hand on her waist. "That's all right, he said." "Are you okay?"

Elizabeth nodded, still not moving.

Matthew felt his own heartbeat accelerate as he pulled her closer. She felt soft against his chest. His eyes dropped to her sweet, soft mouth, he wanted to kiss her. Dare he? He placed his hand on her chin and tipped her head until their eyes met.

Elizabeth relaxed against him and closed her eyes. Matthew lowered his head until his lips brushed hers in a sweet gentle kiss.

Elizabeth felt a warm sensation in her stomach that spread down to her toes, her legs feeling as if they could barely hold her up.

Holding her a bit closer, Matthew kissed her again ever so softly.

"Lizabeth!" called little Chris from the kitchen, interrupting the moment. "Where are you?"

Elizabeth jumped, startled. "I'd better go see what he wants," she whispered, and fled from the pantry.

Matthew stood there a moment, hardly believing what'd just happened. He certainly hadn't planned for it, but she had looked so sweet and all... Well, he couldn't say he regretted it. "I'd better take these down to the basement before someone comes looking for me," he said to himself.

"What took you so long? Did you get lost? "asked Lamar, as Matthew set the buckets down.

"Yes," Matthew answered, turning back to his table and smiling to himself.

"Tell us a story," Bennie and Chris begged as they crawled onto Elizabeth's lap.

Elizabeth opened the book and began reading, but she couldn't concentrate. Her mind was on what had just happened between her and Matthew. Part of her felt warm all over at the memory of their kiss; the other part of her felt ashamed to think of facing him again. What if he now thought she was the kind of girl to allow any guy to kiss her? A wave of condemnation washed over her. I'm only fifteen; what was I thinking? She felt her cheeks burn. What must he think of me? she groaned. What did I get myself into?

The rest of the afternoon passed quickly as everyone worked together, putting the meat in jars and getting it ready to can. But not another word passed between Matthew and Elizabeth.

"You're awfully quiet, Elizabeth," said Leroy, as they drove home that evening.

"I'm just tired," she lied, hoping he didn't suspect anything. She kept silent the rest of the way, lost deep in thought. On one hand she felt a thrill at the memory of their kiss and, on the other, ashamed that she'd let him kiss her so easily. Oh, why is growing up so confusing? she asked herself.

Chapter Eight

Elizabeth was glad when Mom and Dad arrived home from their trip and life got back to normal. It had been a fun experience to see if she could run the household by herself, but it definitely went better with Mom around. She was certainly glad no one had found out about the burnt cookies.

"I think you could plant the flowerbeds today, Elizabeth," said Mom one morning several weeks after they had come back from their trip.

"Oh good," said Elizabeth. What fun it was working outside, especially in the warm spring weather. She sang a little tune as she dug the gardening shovel into the rich black soil.

The April sun shone warmly on her back. It was a perfect day, the birds were chirping, even the air smelled wonderful like sweet little flowers. She certainly didn't envy Marilyn sitting in the schoolhouse teaching every day.

"Hi there, looks like you're busy," said a voice behind her. It was Rachel's brother.

Elizabeth jumped. "Hi Steven, I didn't know anyone was here." She smiled. "What brings you by?"

"I'm afraid I have bad news," he said, picking up the shovel and twisting it nervously in his hands.

"Is Rachel worse?" asked Elizabeth, fearing she already knew the answer.

Steven nodded. "She's back in the hospital." His voice faltered as he tried to hold back the tears. "The doctors aren't giving us much hope this time."

Elizabeth felt as if a great weight were crushing her chest. Surely it wasn't true. Rachel was her best friend. She couldn't die. It wasn't fair. Maybe the doctors were wrong. She wished she could think of something to say to comfort Steven, but no words came out.

"Well, I'd best get going," Steven said at last. "I just thought you'd want to know."

Elizabeth nodded. "Thank you," she said. "I'll go see her as soon as I get a chance."

Steven nodded, then turned and walked back toward his buggy.

Elizabeth sank down in the soft grass beside the tree. Sobs racked her body. She cried until there were no more tears left. The beautiful day had lost its song. It just wasn't fair. Why Rachel?

"Elizabeth," called Mom. "Mrs. Clayton is here."

Elizabeth hurried to get her coat. Mom and Dad had made arrangements for Mrs. Clayton to take her to the hospital to see Rachel.

"Good morning, Elizabeth," Mrs. Clayton smiled as Elizabeth climbed into the car. "How are you this morning?"

"Okay, I guess," answered Elizabeth. "I'm kind of nervous though, I've never been to a hospital before."

"Well, in that case I'll take you in," smiled Mrs. Clayton.

Elizabeth felt as if she had entered another world as they walked through the halls of the hospital. Everywhere she looked there were rooms of people who were sick and in pain.

"Here you are," said Mrs. Clayton. "Room 203. I'll be back after a while."

Elizabeth hesitated before going in. Should she knock? Just then Rachel spotted her.

"Come in," she said. "Don't just stand there."

Elizabeth felt relief wash over her. Rachel sounded fine. Surely she would be okay. She had to be.

"Hi," Elizabeth greeted her warmly. Bending down she kissed her cheek.

"This is such a nice surprise!" Rachel said. "How did you get here?"

"Jill's mom brought me," answered Elizabeth.

The girls sat in silence for several moments. Elizabeth twisted her hands in her lap, not knowing what to say. Should she ask Rachel how she felt? Did she know that they thought she was dying?

"How are you feeling?" she finally blurted out.

"Very weak and tired of fighting this cancer," said Rachel. "Some days are better than others. But let's not talk about that," she changed the subject. "Let's talk about what you've been doing."

"I planted our flower beds," said Elizabeth. "I can hardly wait until they come up."

Rachel nodded. "Mom planted some nice rose bushes and... "Suddenly her voice broke. "I might not be here to see them though," she cried.

Elizabeth reached over and took her hand, noticing how very thin it was. Should she tell Rachel to keep fighting? "Maybe they'll find a cure," she said. "We'll pray for a miracle."

"I hope so." Rachel tried to regain her composure. "I guess as long as there is life there's hope. Right?"

Elizabeth nodded trying hard to think of something else to say. "Guess what we just found out? Nelson and Linda are going to have a baby, and that's not all. She said it might be twins."

Rachel smiled at this news. "I used to always wish I were a twin. But I think you are better than a twin, because you always know how to make me feel better."

Elizabeth gave her a hug. They passed the rest of the time with Elizabeth telling Rachel all the latest happenings in the community.

Finally she said, "I'd best get going."

"Do you have to?" asked Rachel, looking troubled.

"Well, Mrs. Clayton will be here to pick me up soon. Is something wrong?"

"I...well, it's just that I don't like to be alone," Rachel answered. "Too much time to think, I guess. Sometimes I think of what life will like for my family without me... I even think of what my funeral will be like." She began to sob.

"Oh Rachel!" Elizabeth cried, hugging her tightly. "Don't think about that."

"Why did this happen to me?" Rachel continued wiping her eyes. "I've always tried to be good and obey the rules but I'm still scared to die," she whispered.

Elizabeth squeezed her hand. "Maybe you won't," she said.

Rachel didn't seem to be comforted. "We all have to die sometime," she finally said.

Elizabeth left, feeling very low. She may have felt better, however, if she had known what happened in her friend's room later that day.

The day dragged by slowly for Rachel after Elizabeth left. She looked longingly out the window at the beautiful sunset, happy she had a room that looked out over the forests and the hills. If only she could feel as peaceful as the scene before her.

"Hi there," a friendly voice interrupted her thoughts. "May I come in?"

Rachel nodded, wondering who this strange man was.

"Hello, I'm Pastor David Labar," he introduced himself. "I hope you don't mind my stopping by. I come to the hospital twice a week to visit the sick and to pray with them."

Rachel smiled. "That's nice," she said, liking his friendly smile.

"You're Amish, right?" he asked, taking a seat in the chair next to the bed.

Rachel nodded.

"Maybe your pastor has been here already?"

Rachel shook her head.

"I don't want to intrude," the visitor said, "but I really felt as if the Lord was prompting me to come in here tonight and pray with you. May I ask you some questions?"

Rachel nodded, feeling a lump rise in her throat at his kind concern.

"It's Rachel, right?" he asked seeing the name on her tag.

Again Rachel nodded.

"Do you believe in Jesus, Rachel?" he asked.

"Yes," answered Rachel, curious to hear what he was going to say.

Pastor David was silent a moment, asking God to help him know what to say to this girl. He had seen this same look of fear on many sick and dying faces. "Dear Jesus," he prayed silently, "reveal yourself to her, and help her know how much you love her."

"Rachel," he said, looking her straight in the eye, "if you died tonight, do you know for certain that you would go to heaven?"

The tears Rachel had been holding back began to roll down her cheeks. She shook her head. "I don't know," she whispered. "I wish I did though, but I've always been taught that one can only hope."

"Let me read a scripture to you that can help you answer that question." The pastor opened his well worn Bible and began reading: "'These things have I written unto you that believe on the name of the Son of God; that ye may know that ye have eternal life, and that ye may believe on the name of the Son of God.' That's in First John 5:19," he said.

Rachel drank in every word feeling hope rising within her. Could it really be so?

Pastor David continued, "Romans 3:23 says, 'All have sinned and come short of the glory of God.' Do you believe that you have sinned?" he asked.

Rachel nodded through her tears.

"Let me read one more passage to you then," he said. "First John 1: 9 reads, 'If we confess our sins he is faithful and just to forgive us of our sins and to cleanse us from all unrighteousness."

"Could it really be that simple?" Rachel asked in surprise.

"Absolutely," Pastor David smiled. "Could I pray with you?"

Rachel nodded.

"How about if I pray this prayer, and you repeat after me?" he asked.

"I'd like that," said Rachel.

"Dear heavenly Father, Thank you for sending your Son Jesus to die on the cross for my sins. I come before you and confess that I have sinned. I repent of all my sins and I ask that you would forgive me and come into my heart, to be Lord of my life from this day forward. Please cleanse me with your blood and make me your own. In Jesus' name I pray, Amen."

Rachel smiled at the pastor through her tears. She felt as if the weight of the whole world had been lifted off her, replaced by a great joy. Tonight she had found her answer. She was forgiven and God loved her. As she thanked Pastor David for coming, her tears flowed even faster—but this time they were tears of joy.

Chapter Nine

Elizabeth sighed with relief as she hung the last diaper on the line to dry. She was helping Dena for a few days while James was away at a horse auction. With two boys in diapers, doing laundry became a never-ending task.

"It sure is warm for April," said Elizabeth, as she set the empty laundry basket down.

"Yes, it is," agreed Dena. "I see it's starting to look a bit overcast now. It feels like a storm is brewing. I hope the laundry dries before it rains."

"What else are we going to do today?" asked Elizabeth later, as she finished sweeping the laundry room.

"I want to plant the garden this morning, or at least get started." Dena took a worried glance upward.

Although Elizabeth loved the feel of the freshly tilled soil under her feet, she was glad there was only one more row of corn to plant. Her back was getting tired.

"You can take a break, and go in and see if Justin woke up yet," said Dena. Little Solomon had joined his mother and aunt outdoors while his brother slept.

Elizabeth rubbed her stiff muscles and walked toward the house. "The sky is looking much darker than it was an hour ago," she said to herself. "I sure hope we can finish with the planting before it rains." She knew Dena was anxious to have all the work done before the expected little one arrived. With only a week to go before the new arrival, Dena had a busy week ahead of her.

Elizabeth could hear Justin cooing in his crib when she opened the kitchen door. She hurried into the bathroom to wash her hands so that she could rescue him.

Justin smiled excitedly at Elizabeth when she entered the room. "*Naus gae*," he chattered (meaning "go out" in Pennsylvania Dutch). He pointed out the window.

Elizabeth laughed. At fourteen months old, Justin already loved going outdoors. Yes, Dena will sure have her hands full this summer, she thought. Just then a loud clap of thunder shattered the air.

"We better go get your mama," Elizabeth said, hurrying for the door.

She and Dena had barely gathered up the tools and seeds and began heading for the house when a huge bolt of lightning split the sky, and hail began to fall.

"We'd better run," yelled Dena, half dragging Solomon behind her.

Elizabeth was relieved when they were safely in the house. She couldn't remember ever having seen lightning so close or hearing thunder so loud.

"I hope this storm passes soon," said Dena nervously.

"I hope so too," agreed Elizabeth, sitting down with both boys in her lap.

"It's been so warm the past few days." Just then Dena looked out the window. "Oh no!" she gasped. "The barn is on fire!"

Elizabeth flew to the window. "What shall we do?" she cried excitedly.

"Run to the neighbors and have them call the fire department," instructed Dena, "and I'll make sure the animals are all out."

Elizabeth ran through the rain hoping that the neighbors would be home. Lightning must have struck the barn, she realized, and with it full of dry hay, they would have to move fast to salvage anything.

Mrs. Clark, Dena's next door neighbor, answered the door at the first knock. "What's the matter?" she asked. "Is Dena all right?"

Elizabeth tried to catch her breath. "The barn's on fire!" she gasped between breaths. "Could you call the fire department?"

"Yes!" answered Mrs. Clark, running for the phone. "I'll be right over too," she called over her shoulder.

Elizabeth ran back to the barn, hoping it was all a bad dream, but seeing the barn engulfed in flames as she turned in the lane she knew it was real.

"Elizabeth, help!" called Dena when she saw her sister. "The calves are still penned in the barn."

Elizabeth held her apron over her nose and mouth as she crept along the barn floor. The smoke burned her eyes. She felt her way along the barn wall until she reached the calf pen. Reaching up, she felt for the latch and swung it open, praying that the calves would find their way out.

"Elizabeth!" Dena called from the door. "Are you okay?"

"Yes," Elizabeth called back, but she knew the apron she held over her mouth to protect her from the smoke muffled her voice and Dena probably didn't hear her. It seemed to take forever to find her way through the thick cover of smoke. She breathed a sigh of relief when she finally reached the door that led outside.

"I was afraid something happened to you," said Dena in a relieved tone.

Just then they heard the sirens in the distance.

"I'm afraid they won't be able to save it," said Dena near tears. "Oh, I wish we had a way to get hold of James! What a day to be gone."

Elizabeth nodded. She felt dizzy and sick. Maybe she had breathed in more smoke than she thought. She headed for the house; someone had to watch the boys.

Both boys were crying when Elizabeth came through the door.

She held them up to the window to watch the fire trucks drive in the lane. "You're all right," she comforted them. "You were good to obey your mother and stay in the house."

"Will our horses burn up?" asked Solomon, his eyes big with fear.

"No, the animals are okay," Elizabeth reassured them.

The rest of the day passed in a blur. The fireman worked several hours to contain the fire, but in the end, only a smoking heap of charred lumber lay where the old barn had once stood.

Elizabeth was glad when her parents arrived; however, she wished that James would come too. She knew Dena needed his support.

All afternoon relatives, friends, and neighbors stopped by, offering their assistance. And so it was for the next several days. People came bringing food and helping with clean up and other farm work. On Sunday an offering was taken after church for the building of a new barn. Elizabeth knew

Amish were not allowed to carry insurance, but she knew, too, that when someone fell into misfortune everyone was there for each other.

Monday morning arrived bright and clear, and as soon as the sun was up, men began arriving for the barn raising. Their wives came along bringing food. There were casseroles, fried chicken, salads, homemade bread, pies and cookies. Elizabeth counted twenty-five pies on the basement table.

"I feel so unworthy of all this," said Dena, wiping the tears from her eyes.

Mom nodded. "Yah, I know what you mean, but that's why we help when we can and always give our best. Just remember to give it back when someone else has bad luck."

"Yes, we surely will," promised Dena.

In the afternoon all the ladies gathered in the yard to serve refreshments and watch the construction of the new barn. Everywhere Elizabeth looked there was either someone carrying lumber or pounding nails. She thought about what her mother used to say about many hands making light work.

By sunset that evening the last of the rafters were set on the new barn….and at midnight James and Dena were blessed with a healthy baby girl named Kathryn Ann.

Elizabeth sighed with relief when the week ended. A brand new barn stood in place of the old one. The house had gotten cleaned with all the ladies helping, and the boys cleaned the yard, while some of the older ladies finished planting the garden.

"You know I kept asking God 'Why us?' when I saw those flames just eating that old barn," said Dena, looking down at the tiny infant in her arms. "We have had a hard time making ends meet this past year, but now we are even further ahead than we were. You know Uncle Levi brought us two milk cows and several pigs.

"Sometimes I get tired of all the rules, and all the gossiping," she confessed, "but I can tell you some of the people I had held grudges against were the ones who showed up and brought food and gave generously to help with paying for the building materials."

Dena sighed. "I guess what I'm saying is that we all need each other, and the next time I hear gossip about someone I hope I'll remember not to repeat it, but remember the good they've done."

Elizabeth nodded in agreement. She knew she needed to learn the same lesson.

Chapter Ten

Elizabeth sighed with contentment as she curled up on the porch swing with a book. She hadn't even had time to think about reading lately. It seemed longer than two weeks that she'd been at Dena's. So much had happened in that time. She was glad to be back home.

"Mind if I join you?" Marilyn came out on the porch, a bowl of popcorn in her hand.

"Only if you share the popcorn," smiled Elizabeth.

"Don't worry, there's plenty," said Marilyn taking a seat beside her on the swing.

"How much longer until school is out?" asked Elizabeth.

"Only two more weeks," answered Marilyn.

"Are you glad?"

"Yes I guess so, but I enjoyed it."

"I can't even imagine trying to teach school," said Elizabeth.

"Oh, speaking of school," said Marilyn, "Rachel's little sister Christina told me that Rachel was coming home from the hospital today."

"Is she getting better?" asked Elizabeth hopefully.

Marilyn shook her head. "I guess she's home to stay now. There's nothing more they can do."

Elizabeth just sat there staring across the fields, her eyes burning with tears. She had been so busy the past two weeks she hardly had time to think about Rachel. "I guess they weren't wrong, were they?" she said.

"No, I guess not," agreed Marilyn. "Is there anything I can do?"

Elizabeth shook her head. "I'm going to see if Mom will let me go over tomorrow."

"Good idea, said Marilyn. "She needs all the friends she can get right now."

The next afternoon found Elizabeth once again on her way to the Yoder house, struggling with a mixture of fear and dread at seeing Rachel. How did someone look who was dying? She remembered all the things Rachel had said about dying the last time they'd been together. And now it was surely for certain that she was dying. What if it were me? Elizabeth thought. Quickly she tried to push the thought from her mind. If there was one thing she knew for sure, it was that she was not ready to die.

"I've been waiting for this day since the last time you came to see me," said Rachel smiling.

Elizabeth smiled back. Even though Rachel looked weaker, she seemed much better than the last time they were together. Almost happy even.

"How are you feeling?" Elizabeth asked.

"Not too good," said Rachel. "But I feel better about everything else."

Elizabeth was puzzled. Maybe it was a mistake, maybe Rachel found out she really wasn't dying. "What do you mean?" she asked.

Rachel smiled. "So much has happened since we last saw each other." Unable to contain her excitement any longer, Rachel began telling her about her visit with Pastor David at the hospital. Getting out her Bible, she pointed Elizabeth to the same scriptures that the pastor had shown her. "It's all right here," she said.

Elizabeth listened, drinking in every word. Could you really be sure that Jesus forgave you? It must be so; it said it in the Bible. She certainly could see something wonderful had happened to Rachel.

"I just can't tell you how different I feel," said Rachel. "I feel so peaceful."

Elizabeth nodded. She could see that.

"I just feel like the weight of the world has been lifted off me," said Rachel. "I know now that I was looking for something to make feel whole, and there's only one thing that can bring you that feeling. That's Jesus. I longed to be sixteen and have a beau, but..." Her voice grew husky with emotion, "...all that doesn't matter anymore because I probably won't even be here by my sixteenth birthday."

"Oh, Rachel, don't say that," said Elizabeth unable to think of life without her best friend.

Rachel reached out and took Elizabeth's hand. "Won't you say that prayer too?" she asked earnestly.

Nodding her head, Elizabeth slipped down on her knees beside Rachel's bed. Tears streamed down her face as she repeated the sinner's prayer after Rachel.

"Do you feel any different?" asked Rachel, when Elizabeth stood to her feet after the prayer was over.

Elizabeth nodded. "It's hard to explain, but for the first time I can remember Jesus is real to me. I mean, I always knew He was real but now I feel it in my heart. And now I know, it was me He came to die for."

"Happy birthday, Elizabeth," Leroy greeted her when she came to the barn to help with the morning chores. "I can hardly believe you're sixteen."

"Me either," said Elizabeth. She knew that besides a girl's wedding day, this was the most awaited event in a young Amish girl's life. It meant that she could become part of the youth group and begin dating. But somehow all the excitement of that faded when Elizabeth thought of Rachel suffering with cancer.

Leroy wished he knew what to say to make Elizabeth feel better. By the look on her face he guessed she was thinking of her friend. "Are you going to see Rachel today?" he asked.

"Not today," said Elizabeth. "I have to help Mom make supper for tonight. All the family are coming for my birthday supper," she said.

"I want to go over to see Rachel," Elizabeth said to Mom as she put the cookies they had made for the Yoders in a box. "But it's so hard to see her suffer like this."

"I know," Mom sympathized. "But you'll never be sorry you were there for her, no matter how bittersweet it is."

Elizabeth thought about what her mother had said as she drove the familiar road to Rachel's house. It certainly was bittersweet the time they spent together. How different from the not-so-long-ago carefree days at school when tests were their biggest worry.

Elizabeth thought back over her last visit with Rachel and how glad she was that she had prayed and asked Jesus to come into her heart. Everything seemed different now. Even though it was hard to see Rachel suffer, she knew at least now Rachel had hope. She could go to be with Jesus when her life on earth was over.

She thought about Rachel's newfound friends, Pastor David and his wife. They visited Rachel regularly, bringing her flowers or candy, and always encouraging her with Bible verses and praying with her. She was glad Rachel had met them. They were a great source of comfort to the whole Yoder family.

"I brought you some cookies, said Elizabeth, placing the cookies on the little table beside Rachel's bed.

"That's nice," said Rachel unenthusiastically.

"What's wrong?" asked Elizabeth.

"Oh Elizabeth, I'm so upset!" said Rachel. She began to cry. "Do you know who was here last night?" Not waiting for an answer, she went on. "Preacher Jake, that's who! He asked Dad if it was true that an 'English' preacher was coming to our house to pray with me and reading from an 'English' Bible. Dad told him, yes, it was true."

"What happened then?"

"He told Dad that Pastor David and his wife could come and visit, but there should be no more spiritual discussions." Rachel wiped away the tears.

"Oh Rachel, what will you do?" asked Elizabeth, knowing how much those times meant to her.

Rachel shrugged. "What can I do?" she asked.

"I can read to you, and we can pray together," Elizabeth offered.

Rachel smiled., "That'd be nice," she said. "I feel like that's all I have left."

"How was your birthday?" asked Rachel, as the two girls sat talking on the porch swing that afternoon.

"Busy," said Elizabeth. "I helped Mom with the housework, then I mowed the lawn."

"How do you feel?" asked Rachel. "You know it's always been my dream to be sixteen, have a beau, get married and have lots of babies."

Elizabeth smiled, trying to hold back the tears. "Yes, I know," was all she could say.

The two girls sat quietly, not wanting to break the sweet silence. Would this be their last girl chat? Elizabeth wondered.

"Oh I almost forgot," said Rachel. "I got you something for your birthday."

"You shouldn't have," protested Elizabeth.

"It's in my bedroom, in the closet," said Rachel. "Would you mind getting it?"

Elizabeth came back shortly, carrying the gift-wrapped box.

"Go ahead, open it," Rachel urged.

Elizabeth's tears flowed unchecked when she took a Bible from the box and read the message on the inside cover.

To My Best Friend, Elizabeth,

I thought about how I want you to remember me when I'm gone and what could be better than this? I know there will be problems ahead of you in life, so I leave you with this charge: Read this Book every day.

In His love,
Your friend,

Rachel

"Thank you so much," said Elizabeth, hugging her friend. "I know I shall cherish this forever."

The days passed by one by one and the heat of summer was upon them. Knowing that Rachel must be miserable in the hot weather, Elizabeth spent every moment she could with her friend—fanning her, wiping her hot forehead with a cool washcloth, and reading to her from the Bible.

Elizabeth sighed one afternoon as she adjusted the pillow. Poor Rachel was having an extra hard day. Surely she wouldn't go on too much longer suffering like this.

A little moan escaped Rachel's lips. It sounded almost like she was praying. Then Elizabeth caught the last few words: "...in my Father's house are many mansions..." Elizabeth recognized it as verses from John 14, Rachel's favorite biblical passage.

Rachel reached over to take Elizabeth's hand. "I think Jesus is coming for me," she said, gazing toward the ceiling and smiling, as if beholding a beautiful vision.

Elizabeth slipped quietly from the room to summon the family.

"Won't you go with me?" Rachel pleaded looking around at everyone gathered around her bed. "It's so nice there." Her voice was barely audible.

"We'll go with you for as long as you need us," her mother reassured her, taking Rachel's hand.

"That's right," Elizabeth agreed. She knew Rachel wouldn't need them anymore once she was with Jesus.

One by one Rachel's family drew close to the bed and bent down to kiss their daughter and sister goodbye. Elizabeth felt as if her heart would break as she watched Rachel close her eyes and settle back against her pillow, a look of peace and contentment etched across her face. She had gone home to be with Jesus.

Elizabeth leaned against the wall, tears streaming down her face. She heard Mrs. Yoder trying to comfort Rachel's little sisters, telling them, "She's asleep in Jesus' arms now."

Just then a verse from Isaiah came to Elizabeth's mind: "He gathers the lambs and carries them close to his heart."

Chapter Eleven

The late August sun beat warmly down on Elizabeth's back as she finished hoeing the last row of tomatoes.

"It sure is warm today," commented Marilyn, stopping to wipe her forehead with her apron.

"It sure is," agreed Elizabeth. "Muggy too. Maybe we'll have a thunderstorm."

"I know you haven't had an interest in going to the singings since Rachel passed away," Marilyn said slowly, "but I was hoping you'd go with us this Sunday evening."

Elizabeth shrugged. "I guess I always pictured Rachel and I going together," she said.

Marilyn nodded sympathetically. "I understand," she said. "But you've been sixteen almost three months now, and have not gone even once. I've wanted a sister to go with me for a long time," she said wistfully.

Elizabeth gave a faint smile. "Yes, that would be nice. We should do more things together."

Marilyn nodded. She couldn't agree more. Elizabeth certainly had changed a lot this summer she thought, glad they were getting along better. She knew Elizabeth was heartbroken since losing Rachel, but she hoped that going to the singing would help her make new friends and ease her pain.

"Are you ready?" asked Marilyn, knocking on the door to Elizabeth's room Sunday afternoon. "I think Leroy went to hitch up the horse."

"I'll be right there," Elizabeth answered.

She took one last look in the mirror. "Don't be nervous," she said to herself. "Just watch what Marilyn does, and follow her lead." With that thought in mind she grabbed her bonnet and hurried down the stairs.

Several of the girls came out to greet Elizabeth when she arrived. Everyone was friendly and she soon felt at ease. The boys began a lively game of volleyball, while the girls sat around watching the game and visiting.

All too soon the afternoon was over and everyone was summoned inside to eat. After supper was over and dishes washed, the young people gathered in the living room where a long makeshift table had been set up. Boys were seated along one side and girls on the other. The first few hymns were sung in English and the rest of the hymns in German.

After several songs were sung, Elizabeth peeked up from her hymnal. She spotted Leroy sitting at the far end of the table and wondered if he had a special girl in mind. He was twenty-two now, old enough to get married, she thought. She looked at the long row of girls. There were plenty to choose from. Betty Kiem caught her eye. She was tall and slim with light brown hair. Her eyes twinkled when she smiled. She was the prettiest girl there, thought Elizabeth. Maybe someone just needed to point that out to her brother.

"Are you glad you came to the singing tonight?" Leroy asked on their way home.

"Yes, I guess so. Everyone was friendly, but I still felt like I was too young to be with the 'Youngie'," she replied.

"I know what you mean," Leroy said. "I remember feeling that way too, but now I feel like I'm getting too old. There are so many new ones joining the group."

"Old enough to settle down?" asked Elizabeth.

"Oh no!" Leroy groaned. "Let me take a guess: You have found the perfect girl for me in one evening."

"As a matter of fact, there are several likely candidates," Elizabeth responded dryly.

"Well I hope you took down their names," he laughed.

Elizabeth laughed too, almost forgetting how good it felt. She enjoyed the lighthearted banter between her and Leroy.

"It sure is good to hear you laugh," said Leroy. "Rachel would be happy for you."

"I suppose you're right," Elizabeth agreed. "It's just that tonight I kept thinking how much she always had looked forward to being with the 'youngie'."

"That's true," said Leroy, "but I don't think she's missing anything where she's at."

"Make sure you see to it that Linda takes it easy this week," Mom instructed Elizabeth on Monday morning. Elizabeth was going to spend the week helping Linda get ready to host the church service at their house the coming Sunday.

Elizabeth nodded. "I'll try," she promised. But she knew it wouldn't be easy. Linda was almost seven months pregnant with the twins, and this was also her first time to host a church service. Getting ready for that, and the arrival of the twins, was keeping her busy. She always wanted everything to be just perfect, and her mother had reason to be concerned that her daughter would overdo.

"I am so glad you could make it!" said Linda greeted Elizabeth at the door.

"Me, too," said Elizabeth. She had been looking forward to spending time with Linda. Maybe she would get to see Nancy too. She hadn't seen her since Nelson and Linda had gotten married.

After a tall glass of iced tea and getting caught up on what was happening at home, Elizabeth was ready to get started. "What shall I do first?" she asked, tying on her apron. "Mom said to see to it that you take it easy this week, so tell me what's to be done and you just rest."

"I'll try," said Linda "but I'm afraid there's more work than you'll be able to do by yourself."

Elizabeth wasn't afraid of hard work; in fact, she rather enjoyed a challenge. She busied herself doing laundry, washing all the bedding and curtains. Next there were windows to wash and the lawn to mow, and by nine o'clock that evening Elizabeth was dead to the world.

The next day started out the same. There wasn't a stone left unturned. Every nook and cranny was cleaned.

"Do you think you could go to town for me this afternoon?" asked Linda on Wednesday morning.

"I don't know if I know the way," Elizabeth answered.

"I'll see if Nancy could go with you," Linda said.

"It sure is nice to see you again," said Elizabeth, as she and Nancy were on their way to town later that day. Nancy was exactly as Elizabeth remembered her—every hair neatly in place.

She listened as Nancy told her all about how she had gotten together with Eugene. They had begun dating as soon as she Nancy had turned sixteen.

"How about you?" asked Nancy. "Have you had a date?"

Elizabeth shook her head. She couldn't even imagine dating anyone yet.

"Maybe we can set you up with a date this weekend," Nancy said. "There are lots of cute guys around here."

"I don't think 'cute' qualifies for a good date," Elizabeth answered.

Nancy laughed. "You are something else! Surely it couldn't hurt to date a few guys just for fun."

Elizabeth thought a moment before answering. Dating for fun did not appeal to her at all.

"Here we are," said Nancy, driving up to the hitching rack.

Elizabeth was glad she'd been spared an answer. She didn't want to hurt Nancy's feelings but, at the same time, she couldn't imagine dating just for fun. It didn't seem like the right thing to do.

"I'll go to over to that department store while you go get your groceries," Nancy said, pointing to a store across the street.

"I'll try to hurry," Elizabeth promised.

Once inside the store she pulled the long list from her purse and began filling her cart: butter, eggs, cheese, peanut butter. The list was never ending.

She sighed with relief when the last item was crossed off the list. "I hope I didn't forget anything," she said to herself, as she piled the groceries onto the checkout lane.

"Need a hand?" asked a voice behind her.

Elizabeth spun around. "Matthew!" she said surprised. "I didn't know you were here."

"What are you doing all the way over here?" he asked.

"I'm staying at Linda's this week," Elizabeth replied.

Their conversation was interrupted as the clerk finished tallying up her bill. Paying for the groceries, Elizabeth quickly hurried out the store.

Matthew followed her. "If I wouldn't know better I'd think you're trying to get away from me," he teased, his eyes twinkling mischievously.

Elizabeth blushed. "Should I be?"

Matthew laughed. "Here, let me do that" he offered, setting the bags of groceries into the back of the buggy.

"Will you be at the singing Sunday evening?" he asked.

"Yes, I guess so. I've only been to one so I feel kinda strange. I don't know anyone but Nancy and Marilyn and Leroy." Elizabeth stopped. He must think I'm an idiot for rambling on so, she thought to herself.

Finishing up with the groceries, Matthew came over to stand beside her. "You know me, don't you?" he asked.

Elizabeth looked up and their eyes met. "Yes," she answered, suddenly feeling very shy.

"Would you like to get to know me better?" His eyes held her gaze.

Elizabeth felt almost nigh to panic. He looked as if he might kiss her right there on the spot.

Matthew grinned, as if reading her mind. Bending down closer, he whispered in her ear, "Don't worry, I won't kiss you right here, although the thought has crossed my mind."

"How do you know I'd let you?" she asked.

Matthew chuckled. "Shall we find out?" he asked, stepping closer.

Elizabeth, at a loss for words, shook her head.

"I'm sorry for teasing you," said Matthew, reaching over and taking her hand.

Elizabeth felt her heart skip a beat at his touch.

"I've been wanting to ask you something for a long time, I was wondering if—"

"Hi there, you two," said Nancy, coming around the buggy and interrupting Matthew's question.

Elizabeth turned and quickly busied herself with untying the horse, not sure if she was relieved or disappointed at the interruption. She listened as Nancy chatted with Matthew in her easy outgoing manner.

"Will you be at the singing Sunday night?" Nancy asked.

"I wouldn't miss it," he said, winking at Elizabeth before turning and walking away.

"Aren't you going to tell me what that was all about?" asked Nancy, as soon as they were both seated in the buggy and driving away.

"What what was about?" asked Elizabeth, feigning innocence.

"You and Matthew, that's what!" said Nancy. "I know there was something going on when I walked up on you two. Did he ask you for a date?"

"No, he did not."

"Well, I saw how you two were looking at each other so I know there's something going on. Don't tell me there's not."

"Then I won't," said Elizabeth laughing.

Knowing she wasn't going to get an answer, Nancy reluctantly dropped the subject.

In bed that night, Elizabeth's mind went over her encounter with Matthew a thousand times. Was he going to ask her for a date? What would she say if he did? She remembered her conversations with Rachel about dating. She knew she didn't want to date just for fun like many of the young people in the youth group did. Finding a life partner was a solemn matter. Although she was attracted to Matthew, she was only sixteen and not ready for a commitment. And how did she know Matthew was serious?

"Help me, Lord," she prayed, "to know what your will is for my life. Help me to seek you above all else." Feeling the matter settled in her heart, she turned over and blew out the lamp. "Better get to sleep," she said to herself. Tomorrow was Sunday and she knew it would be a long day.

The church service was over, and Elizabeth hurried to help get the food set out on the tables. She listened as the older ladies sat around visiting. It was then she found out that Matthew had left by train for Montana on Saturday to go help his uncle who had been injured in a farm accident.

"How long will he be gone?" she heard one of the ladies inquire of Matthew's mother.

"Well, I think he plans to stay until Christmas," answered Mrs. Yoder.

"My, that's a long time,' commented the other lady. "I reckon it's a good thing he doesn't have a girl to leave behind."

"Yes, I suppose so," agreed Mrs. Yoder. "Lamar and Edwin have girls," she said, referring to Matthew's older brothers. "But you know Matthew. I don't know if he'll ever get serious and settle down. I think he has itchy feet, and wants to travel first."

Elizabeth smiled as she listened to the ladies going on to another topic. In her heart she felt a sense of relief that she wouldn't have to answer Matthew's question tonight.

"The 'youngie' are getting together at our house this afternoon," Nancy told Elizabeth when they'd finished washing the dishes after lunch. "Want to join us?"

"Sure, that sounds like fun," Elizabeth agreed.

"Have you met Rosemary and Sharon?" asked Nancy as the two girls joined them on their walk to Nancy's house.

Elizabeth shook her head. "No, I haven't," she smiled. Sharon and Rosemary smiled back.

"We figured out who you were this morning though," said Rosemary. "You look so much like your sister Linda."

Both girls were friendly and Elizabeth immediately felt at ease with them. She listened as they talked about the dates they had the night before and who was dating whom. Elizabeth was surprised with the openness and ease with which they discussed such matters. As far as she knew, in their community girls didn't even talk about their current steady boyfriend.

But an even greater surprise was in store for her when she reached Nancy's house. Several buggies were parked on the lawn with a cluster of young people gathered around them. Most of the boys had gathered around a buggy that had music coming from inside, and as they drew closer, she spotted two girls sitting inside with beers in hand, laughing and joking with the guys.

Elizabeth could hardly believe her eyes. She knew their church leadership would never tolerate such going-ons! She tried not to let her surprise show when two more girls appeared, walking across the lawn, smoking cigarettes. She had heard this was a rowdy group of young people but to see 'youngie' drinking and smoking was a bit of a shock! The couples that were dating stood around holding hands and talking.

Elizabeth almost laughed out loud. This would simply be unheard of at home. At their singing the boys and girls didn't associate with each other. But in the end, Elizabeth had to admit she had enjoyed her afternoon. Everyone had been very laid back and friendly, guys and girls alike. No one seemed to notice or mind that she had refused the drinks and cigarettes offered her.

Elizabeth's feet ached that night as she climbed the stairs up to her room. She certainly was glad to be back home. She reflected back over her week, and all that had happened, as well as all she had seen and heard that afternoon. She wished she could talk it over with Rachel. Her heart ached with loneliness for her friend. She missed not having someone to share her thoughts and feelings with.

Stretching out on her bed, she reached over on the nightstand and picked up her Bible. Letting it fall open at random, her eyes fell on Philippians 2:15, a verse she'd underlined some time ago: "That ye may be blameless and harmless, the sons of God in the midst of a crooked and perverse nation, among whom ye shine as lights in the world."

With a thankful heart Elizabeth closed her Bible and prayed, "Dear Lord Jesus, thank you for keeping me from doing something I would later have been ashamed of. Help me be a light to those around me. Help me to live that they will see you in me. Amen."

Elizabeth paused from her raking for a moment. She loved this time of the year. She watched as a gentle breeze came and carried away some of the leaves she'd just finished raking.

"Need a hand?" called Anna, coming across the lawn waving her rake.

"I sure do," answered Elizabeth, happy to see help arrive. With their big yard, raking seemed like a never-ending job.

"You are always coming to help us so we thought we'd surprise you and come give you a hand."

Elizabeth's heart warmed toward her sister in-law. She knew it was a sacrifice for Anna to come help her. With three little ones and another one on the way, Anna had her hands full.

"Mom wanted to make sure the yard is raked before I have to go help Linda," Elizabeth said.

The two visited as they worked.

"We got a letter from Matthew the other day," said Anna. "He says he is enjoying himself so much, he may stay longer. He did say, too, that he missed everyone so we'll see.

"I can't imagine being gone from home that long," said Elizabeth.

"I remember when Daniel and I first got married and moved over here, I got lonesome for home a lot until our first baby was born."

"How old were you when you and Daniel started dating?" asked Elizabeth curiously.

"We were both eighteen," answered Anna.

"Was it love at first sight?"

Anna laughed, "I don't think there is such a thing. I believe loves grows over a period of time." Then she asked, "How about you? Is there anyone special in your life?"

Elizabeth shook her head. "I'll probably end up an old maid," she laughed.

"Well, there's a saying that it's better to be happily unmarried than to be unhappily married," said Anna.

Elizabeth agreed.

Several days later the long awaited message arrived. Nelson and Linda had twin boys, Jonathan and Joshua.

Elizabeth hurried to pack her suitcase. Linda had asked if, after the babies were born, Elizabeth could come be the nursemaid for the first two weeks.

Dad and Mom accompanied Elizabeth over to Nelson and Linda's, anxious to meet the newest members of the Hostetler clan.

"Oh, aren't they cute?" cooed Elizabeth as she and Mom inspected the tiny babies, each of them weighing barely five pounds.

How are you ever going to tell them apart?" Elizabeth asked. To her they looked exactly alike with their little red faces and black hair.

"They put name bracelets on them at the hospital," said Nelson, "so they'll wear those until we figure out distinguishing characteristics."

"If you look closely, "Linda pointed out, "you'll see that Joshua has a tiny birthmark on his arm. It'll fade away, but for now it will help us tell them apart."

"This makes eight grandchildren for us," said Dad, sounding pleased. He enjoyed the grandchildren as much as he did their own children. "The Lord has certainly blessed us." smiling fondly at his wife.

"Yah, He sure has," Mom agreed.

Elizabeth's days were filled with crying babies and mounds of dirty diapers. Then there was bath time and feedings.

"I don't think I could count all the people that have come to see these precious little guys," said Linda one afternoon as she and Elizabeth rocked the babies to sleep. "Nelson and I have sure appreciated all you've done for us. I don't know how I'll manage once you go home."

"I know I'll sure miss these little guys," said Elizabeth, kissing Jonathan's forehead.

"It sure is nice to have you home again," said Mom. "It gets kinda lonely around here with you and Marilyn both gone."

Elizabeth hadn't thought about Mom missing her company. Although she and Mom still sometimes had an occasional disagreement over the church rules, Elizabeth realized how much she had also missed her mother. "I'm glad to be home too," she said.

Mom smiled as she listened to Elizabeth talk about taking care of the twins. It was hard to believe that her youngest was now seventeen. "It doesn't seem like that long ago that you were that age and look at you now, a young lady all grown up." Mom's voice sounded a little sad. "It makes me feel old."

Elizabeth glanced over at her mother, taking note of the graying hair at her temples. She never thought about Mom feeling old.

"Dad hired a driver to go to Laporte on Saturday to go Christmas shopping," Mom said, changing the subject.

"Oh good," Elizabeth smiled. "I can hardly wait."

Chapter Twelve

Christmas was over and the winter days dragged on.

"This winter seems so long to me," said Elizabeth, as she and Marilyn donned coats one night and headed out for an evening walk.

"I think the kids at school feel the same way," agreed Marilyn.

"Last year this time I was spending a lot of time with Rachel," said Elizabeth. "I wonder what this year holds."

Marilyn nodded, "Me too."

"Oh, just look at that sunset," said Elizabeth interrupting. "I could just stand here and look at it forever."

"You go right ahead then, said Marilyn. "I'm going back in. I'm freezing."

Elizabeth brushed the snow off a nearby log and took a seat to watch the beautiful sight before her. The hues of gold, pink and lavender appeared to have been brushed in streaks across the sky. Elizabeth sighed a sigh of content-ment, realizing anew that the God who made this sunset loved her. She thought about Rachel now on the other side of that sunset—free of pain. Perhaps even now she was playing in the river of life or skipping on streets of gold. The thought made Elizabeth smile. Maybe Mom was right; time could heal broken hearts.

"Are you about ready, Elizabeth?" Mom called up the stairs. "Dad is bringing the horse up for you."

Elizabeth slipped into her coat and hurried down the stairs. She was on her way to help Anna with some sewing. "Save some cookies for me," she threw over her shoulder as she hurried out the door, ran through the snow, and hopped into the waiting buggy.

"Charlie is going lame so I thought you could take Champ," Dad handed her the reins. "But be careful," he warned. "He's a bit high strung."

"I'll be careful," Elizabeth promised.

Elizabeth enjoyed the challenge of driving Champ and was glad Dad trusted her with him. She loved the sound of the snow crunching underneath the steel wheels of the buggy and the feel of the wind in her face as they raced along.

"Are you sure it's safe for Elizabeth to drive that horse?" asked Mom anxiously when her husband came back into the house. "He's got a lot of spunk."

"Probably no more than Elizabeth," Dad laughed. "You worry too much. She'll be fine."

"I hope you're right," Mary replied, "but I can't help but feel a bit uneasy."

"Dad was right," Elizabeth said aloud. "Champ certainly is full of spunk!" She tightened her grip a bit on the reins as the horse kept trying to pick up speed.

Suddenly, two deer came out of nowhere and leapt across the road directly in front of them.

Champ snorted and darted sharply to the left, breaking into a gallop.

Elizabeth pulled hard on the reins but to no avail. Bracing her feet hard against the dash, she pulled with all her might. "Whoa Champ!" she said loudly. "Whoa Boy!" She tried to keep her voice calm, but the horse continued to pick up speed. She began to panic. They were coming up to a busy four corners and there was no slowing him down.

Elizabeth braced her feet hard against the dash in one last effort to stop him. "Oh Lord, please be with me. Don't let there be any traffic," she prayed." Pulling hard on the right rein, she tried to guide Champ into a snow bank at the corner. Then she looked up. There was a truck coming—and Champ wasn't turning!

Taking the last pan of cookies from the oven, Mom sighed. She couldn't seem to shake her feeling of heaviness. "David is right; I do worry too much," she said to herself. Knowing there was one thing that always calmed her and made her feel better, she took her little black prayer book, headed for the bedroom, and shut the door.

"I wonder why Elizabeth isn't here yet?" said Anna, looking out the window again. "Mom said she'd be here by nine o'clock."

"Its only nine-forty," said Daniel, looking at his pocket watch. "She probably just got a late start."

"I reckon you're right," said Anna. "No need to worry."

"How many cookies can I have?" Leroy teased, smiling at Mom.

Mom smiled back. "Eleven less than a dozen," she answered, putting the pan in the sink.

Leroy laughed. "But these are my favorite," he protested.

Just then there was a knock at the door.

"Could you see who that is, Leroy?"

Leroy looked out the window. "It's the police," he announced.

Mom felt her legs go weak. Something must have happened to Elizabeth!

"Is Mr. or Mrs. Hostetler here?" Mom heard the uniformed officer ask Leroy.

"Yes. Won't you step inside?" Leroy held the door open a bit wider.

The officer stepped inside and removed his hat. "Mrs. Hostetler," he said, "I'm afraid I have bad news. There's been an accident down at Reeds four corners, and we believe your daughter was involved. Do you know if that is a possibility?"

Mother nodded. She felt as if her lungs were running out of air. "Is she okay?" she asked, afraid to hear his answer.

"She's in good hands, Mrs. Hostetler," he reassured her.

"Did they take her to the hospital in Laporte?" Leroy asked.

The officer shook his head. "No sir, she has been airlifted to Williamsport."

"Oh Leroy," Mom cried, "go and get Dad—and hurry!"

Mom quickly changed into a clean dress, her hands trembling as she pinned on her cape and apron. Over and over she recited a prayer from the little black book she had been reading a short time before. "Help us, O Lord, our helper; rescue us in time of trouble," she prayed.

"Are you ready?" Leroy called from kitchen.

"I'll be out in a minute," she replied, grabbing her shawl and bonnet.

"I've made arrangements for Randy down the road to take you to Williamsport," Leroy told his mother. "He said he'd be right over. And Mrs. Clayton will bring the rest of us this afternoon."

Leroy watched with a heavy heart as his parents drove out the lane. Oh, if only they wouldn't have let her drive Champ!

"Leroy is here," said Anna looking out the window. "I wonder what he wants?"

She was soon to find out. "Is Elizabeth going to be all right?" she asked, after hearing the reason for Leroy's visit.

Leroy shrugged, "All we know is that she was hit by a truck at Reeds Four Corners and was airlifted to Williamsburg hospital."

"It doesn't sound good," said Daniel worriedly. "Is there room for us to go with you?"

"Yes," Leroy assured him. "That's why Mrs. Clayton brought her van. She thought you all might want to go along."

"Can we drop off the children at my parents on the way?" asked Anna.

"That's fine," said Leroy, picking up Bennie and putting his coat on.

Soon everyone was rounded up from their various homes, and they were on their way.

"What happened to the horse?" asked Dena.

"The police officer said he was broken up quite badly, so they had to put him down," Leroy replied.

The ninety-minute drive seemed like an eternity. Everyone was lost in their own thoughts, and praying that their sister would be okay. Upon arriving at the hospital, they learned that Elizabeth was still in surgery.

"I'm so glad you all could come," said Mom. "It's a great comfort having you all here."

"Shall we have prayer?" Dad asked. Everyone nodded, and he ushered them into a little chapel down the hall. Upon entering, the men removed their hats and Mom sobbed softly into her handkerchief. "Oh Lord," she prayed silently, "please let her be okay."

"Are you the Hostetlers?" A short gray-haired man approached them.

"Yes," said Dad rising to his feet. "Can you tell us anything?"

"I'm Dr. Taylor," the man introduced himself, shaking Dad's hand. He then filled them in on Elizabeth's injuries. There were several broken bones including four broken ribs and a punctured lung. "But our biggest concern at the moment is the bump on her head," he continued. "She has not regained consciousness. I'm sorry to bring you this news," he said kindly. If there's any change, I'll let you know. Keep praying." He laid hand on Dad's shoulder.

"Can we see her?" asked Mom.

"Yes, but just for a few minutes," he cautioned.

Mom and Dad slowly approached the bed. Hardly believing the pale girl lying there was their Elizabeth, Mom reached out and gently touched her hand. She looked at the tubes and machines attached to her, feeling very helpless. What could they do?

"Elizabeth," Mom said quietly, trying to hold back the tears, "Dad and I are here now, and you are going to be all right."

Their tears flowed unchecked. Oh, if only there was something they could do. It seemed like a bad dream.

Moving to the side of the bed, the nurse signaled to them that their time was up. Mom turned and took one last look as she wiped the tears from her eyes and left the room. It was all in God's hands now. They could only wait and pray.

Making their way back to the waiting room, Dad and Mom joined the rest of the children who were full of questions. Will she be all right? was the question on everyone's lips. Their faces were anxious as Dad described how frail and helpless their sister looked in her hospital bed, hooked up to various machines.

"She's young and strong," said Leroy at last. "She'll be okay." He wished he were half as sure of that as he sounded.

The night seemed to last forever. Everyone had opted to stay at the hospital with Dad and Mom. They sat around drinking coffee, trying to stay awake, and reminiscing about the day Elizabeth was born, the day she fell off the pony…the list went on and on. And now here she was a young lady. But everyone kept coming back to the accident. What could've happened? Did Elizabeth pull out in front of the truck? It didn't sound like her. She was always cautious. There were so many unanswered questions.

"I should've listened to Mom," said Dad regretfully. "She was uneasy about having Elizabeth drive Champ."

"Don't feel like that," Mom said gently. "Maybe this all happened for a reason."

Just then the doctor appeared. "You have a mighty fine family here." He smiled at Dad.

Dad nodded. "Yes, we have been truly blessed," he agreed.

"I just checked in on Elizabeth and she is in stable condition. Her vital signs are good; however, she hasn't regained consciousness yet. We are hopeful that will happen soon."

"Can I go in to see her?" Mom asked.

"Yes, I think that would be fine," the doctor replied.

Mom entered the room and laid her hand on Elizabeth's forehead. "Elizabeth," she said softly, "it's time to wake up now. Everyone has been here all night, even Linda's twins." Mom continued talking softly, watching closely for any sign of movement.

Elizabeth's eyelids felt heavy. She could hear her mother calling her. Was it time to get up? She tried to open her eyes again. There was Mom. Why was she crying? Her head was hurting. "Maybe I'll just sleep a little longer," she thought, letting her eyes fall shut again.

"Elizabeth! Elizabeth!" Mom said, louder now. "Can you hear me?"

The nurse who had been standing on the far side of the room hurried over to the bed. "I think someone may be waking up," she smiled. "I'll go get the doctor."

"The rest of you may as well go home," said Dad that afternoon. "The doctor says Elizabeth's improving, and if we need anything we'll let you know."

"We'll be back tomorrow evening," said Leroy, reluctant to leave. "Let us know if there's any change."

"I hope the children were no bother," said Anna, putting the boys' boots on.

"They were no trouble," her mother reassured her. "We enjoyed having them." Then she asked, "How's Elizabeth doing? Do the doctors think she'll be okay?"

"They are more hopeful today," answered Anna. "She opened her eyes this morning. This has really made me realize how much she means to me," she added thoughtfully. "She's always such a willing worker, and has helped me out so much."

She listened as Dad and Leroy asked Matthew all about his hunting trip. She was glad Leroy approved of Matthew. She had never talked to Dad or Mom about whether or not they approved, but since they hadn't said anything negative, she supposed that was a good sign.

"What about you?" asked Matthew, turning to look at her. "Did you get a deer?"

"We can have prayer to return thanks for the food," smiled Dad, "and then she can take you out to the shop and show you."

As soon as prayers were over, Matthew and Elizabeth headed out for the shop. "Alone at last," Matthew said, taking her in his arms. Holding her close, he bent his head to kiss her.

"I missed you," she hugged him back.

"Me too, I'm glad to be back. Now, don't keep me in suspense any longer. I want to see your deer."

Elizabeth led him to the back of the shop where Leroy had mounted the antlers and hung them up on the wall.

"Wow, did you really get this?" exclaimed Matthew.

Elizabeth nodded, "But I'll have to admit it wasn't as easy as I thought it would be, although I could never admit that to Leroy," she added.

Matthew's sides ached from laughing as Elizabeth recounted exactly how she had gotten the deer. She even told him about her black eye.

"You'll never hear the end of that," he warned.

"I've already found that out," she agreed.

The rest of the day passed by quickly as they played board games with the family and got caught up on all that happened in their time apart. Elizabeth wished the day could go on forever. She loved spending time with Matthew.

After everyone else had retired for the evening, Matthew and Elizabeth settled down on the living room sofa watching the soft shadows made by the small oil lamp and enjoying the quiet camaraderie between the two of them.

"Next Sunday it'll be nine months that we've been dating," commented Elizabeth. "I remember how nervous I was the first time you came to see me."

"So was I," Matthew chuckled, as he remembered back to that day. "I had waited so long to ask you I was afraid someone else had beat me to it."

"Several others had asked me, but I was waiting for you," she admitted.

Hearing that Matthew pulled her close and kissed her tenderly. "I want you to know that I hope someday you will be my wife."

"Is that a proposal?"

"Absolutely," Matthew smiled. "Will you marry me?"

"Yes!" Elizabeth felt like she was floating on a cloud and would never come down.

Elizabeth watched the snowflakes fall lazily to the ground. It was once again the Christmas season.

"Want to go for a walk?" asked Marilyn, interrupting her thoughts.

"Sure!" Elizabeth loved going for walks, but Marilyn wasn't usually the one to suggest it, so she knew something was up.

Donning coats and scarves the two girls headed out into the snowy afternoon.

"Isn't it pretty out here?" commented Elizabeth. "It looks like a winter wonderland."

"Yes, it sure does," Marilyn agreed. "I don't get outside much anymore since I've started teaching school."

"Is there something on your mind?" asked Elizabeth.

Marilyn was quiet a moment before answering. "Yes, actually there are a couple things I wanted to talk to you about." She cleared her throat nervously.

"Did someone ask you for a date?" guessed Elizabeth.

Marilyn grinned sheepishly. "That's part of it."

"Who?"

"It's Steven Yoder," Marilyn answered.

"Oh, please tell me you said yes," begged Elizabeth.

Marilyn nodded. "We're having our first date this Sunday."

"Oh, I think that's great." Elizabeth sighed happily. "He's very nice and you deserve someone nice."

"I don't see how you can say that," said Marilyn, "after the way I've treated you in the past. I've always been jealous of you," she went on to confess, "and, as a result, I know I often haven't been very kind toward you or made life easy for you. I was jealous that you were thinner and prettier than me. Then along came Matthew and you had a boyfriend before me too."

She stopped walking and turned toward Elizabeth. "I just want to confess these things to you and ask for your forgiveness."

"Oh, Marilyn," Elizabeth replied, shocked at her sister's admission. "I had no idea you felt that way, but I have to apologize for not being nice to you either. And as for being prettier, Marilyn that's just not true!" Elizabeth protested. "You don't give yourself enough credit. I accept your apology if you can forgive me too?"

Marilyn nodded, taking out her hanky and wiping away her tears. "I would like for us to have a better relationship. The other night I was reading about jealousy being sin and I just knew I had to confess to you how I felt."

Elizabeth nodded. "I need to confess that whenever we had a fight I would always go and tell Leroy, and talk bad about you behind your back to him. I'm sorry."

"I can't tell you how much better I feel," said Marilyn as the two headed back toward the house.

"Same here," agreed Elizabeth. "I hope things will be different between us from now on."

Elizabeth stayed outside for a long time after Marilyn had gone into the house. She felt like a huge weight had lifted from her. It was certainly true that confession was good for the soul and she hoped that she would always remember that.

It was Christmas day and everyone had gathered in the living room to open presents. Elizabeth looked around. She loved watching the little one's faces as they opened their packages. What could be better than family? Then she looked over at Matthew sitting beside Leroy on the couch. How well he fit in with her family.

"Elizabeth, it's your turn now," said Dena, pushing a big box in front of her.

"Oh, this is too much," said Elizabeth, holding up a delicate china saucer with tiny pink flowers. There's a whole set in here!" Opening the card she read: "Many thanks for all your help. Merry Christmas, signed, Daniel and Anna, James and Dena, Nelson and Linda.

"Oh, I'm not worth all that," she said. Then, as she opened the rest of her gifts, she exclaimed, "Oh, there's more!" There were matching serving bowls and platters from Dad and Mom and a water set to match from Matthew.

"I'm afraid I can't take any credit," said Matthew, grinning sheepishly. "I just went along with the crowd."

And so the rest of the afternoon continued until the entire living room floor was covered with paper and boxes. Another Christmas was over.

Chapter Eighteen

Elizabeth shivered, tucking the buggy robe a little tighter around her legs to keep out the cold winter wind. "I am glad Dena lives only three miles away," she said, "else we'd freeze before we get there."

"Yah, I'll sure be glad when this cold spell ends," agreed Mom. "Dad is even thinking of taking another trip to Florida if this keeps up."

"That sounds mighty inviting on a day like today," said Elizabeth. She and Mom were going over to help Dena clean her house and prepare the food for Sunday services being held there this Sunday.

Several other ladies had already arrived and were busy cleaning when Mom and Elizabeth walked in the door.

"What can I do to help?" asked Elizabeth, tying her white apron around her slim waist.

"I thought maybe you could start in the bedroom," said Dena, handing her a list and a bucket of cleaning supplies.

Elizabeth made her way into the bedroom. Sitting on the edge of the bed she began reading the list of instructions: wash windows, polish furniture…She stopped reading when she heard her name mentioned in the next room.

"Yah, it don't surprise me one bit," she heard a voice say that she recognized as Dorothy Miller's. "Elizabeth was always just too fancy for our youngie."

"I hear she don't even come to the hymn singings in our community anymore," added Edna Bontreger.

"Our Harley asked her for a date once," continued Dorothy, "and she turned him down. He was heartbroken, but I told him beauty is only skin deep. And now she's dating that Matthew Yoder. Why with that fancy haircut he's got, I don't even know how he can call himself Amish."

"Yah you are right," agreed Edna. "They are getting so liberal over there in that community. I just said to Henry last night I believe the day will come when we will not even associate with them anymore."

Elizabeth gasped. She could hardly believe what she was hearing! How horrible! What had she done to them anyway? Grabbing the pail of soapy water and a rag, she began to scrub the mopboards. She felt more like going over to the adjoining bedroom and giving those two ladies a piece of her mind.

The conversation in the other room soon turned to rumors of some of the other ladies present that day, and Elizabeth turned back to the task at hand, fuming silently as she worked. How cruel! Who did they think they were? Edna and Dorothy had long had a reputation for being gossips, so why didn't the church leadership confront them? Elizabeth wondered. The Bible clearly said gossiping was sin.

"Oh, Matthew," said Elizabeth that Sunday evening, once they settled down at the kitchen table, "I can't tell you how awful I felt listening to those two go on so!" She recounted the conversation she'd over overheard at Dena's.

"I know once you become a church member you have to make a confession before the church for breaking the rules, like buying material for a dress that's not allowed. But I have never heard of anyone having to make a confession for slandering or gossiping!"

Mathew had never seen Elizabeth so upset about anything before. "I know what you mean, he said at last. "I've complained to Dad about things like that too, but he always just says I shouldn't worry about what others say and do, just make sure I do what's right."

Elizabeth was silent. She felt like she had just received a rebuke, a much-needed one too. Here she had been so concerned about bringing Dorothy and Edna and their ever-wagging tongues to justice, when the Bible said to pull the beam from your own eye first. Elizabeth felt ashamed. If she had gone to the Lord in prayer, she could've known that for herself. She had just confessed to Marilyn recently that at times she had talked about her behind her back. Yes, she had a long way to go in that area herself. She would have to remember that the next time she was tempted to talk about someone.

"You're awfully quiet," observed Matthew. "Did I say something wrong?"

"No, you were right in what you said," answered Elizabeth, "but I still wish they knew how much their gossiping hurt others.

"Are you planning on joining the instruction class for baptism?" asked Matthew, changing the subject.

Elizabeth shrugged. "I don't know," she said. "There are so many things I don't understand and some of those I do, I don't quite agree with."

"Oh Elizabeth, I can't imagine not being Amish. I know they aren't perfect but what religion is?"

"I know you are right," said Elizabeth, "but I think it also takes more than just being Amish."

"What do you mean?" asked Matthew.

"Well, I just think it seems like some people feel as long as they obey all our rules, they are right before God."

"And you don't think they are?" Matthew inquired.

Elizabeth shrugged, "I guess it's not for me to judge." She thought about a verse she'd read in Isaiah 64:6 that said all our righteousness is as filthy rags. She knew it was only the blood of Jesus that could wash away sins and make a person right before God.

Matthew changed the subject to other topics but he couldn't help but notice how quiet Elizabeth was the rest of the evening.

Matthew thought about their conversation as he went to work the next morning. What had Elizabeth meant when she said it took more than just being Amish? Did she think Amish people weren't Christians? He knew most of them prayed out of their prayer books everyday and went to church every other Sunday. In fact, some went every Sunday. They would have to talk more about it he decided.

"My, am I ever glad to see you!" said Dena, greeting Elizabeth at the door Monday morning.

"Yah, Mom thought you would be," said Elizabeth. "That's why she sent me. I guess she remembers what a big job it is to clean up after Sunday services."

The two soon busied themselves with the clean up, mopping floors and setting furniture back in place.

"You're awfully quiet," remarked Dena as they worked. "Is something wrong?"

"I've just got a lot on my mind," Elizabeth said, not sure if she should tell Dena what it was.

"Want to talk about it?"

"Well, it all started last week when I came over to help," Elizabeth began, telling Dena how she'd overheard Dorothy and Edna's conversation and ending with the discussion she and Matthew had had the night before.

"James and I have struggled with lots of questions like that too," confided Dena.

"Have you found any answers?" asked Elizabeth hopefully. She'd never talked to Dena again about their conversation that day at the hospital.

"I'm sure we will never know all the answers," Dena admitted, "but after we talked at the hospital last winter I began thinking about what God meant to me. I was praying to Him but it was out of habit. I repeated the same prayers every day, never thinking what the words meant or what I was saying. And yet I thought that I was right before God, because I kept all the rules.

"On the outside I looked okay," she went on, "but when we had that fire, I did a lot of thinking. I wanted to make sure I looked good on the outside, but I didn't spend time making sure my heart was right. I would feel bad against James when things didn't go my way. I would talk about some of the people in church that I didn't like. The list goes on. And then one day I read a verse in the Bible that made me stop and think."

"What was it?" Elizabeth interrupted.

"I was reading Luke eleven when I came to verse thirty nine." She picked up her Bible and read: "'The Lord said unto him, now ye Pharisees ye make clean the outside of the cup and the platters, but your inward part is full of greed and wickedness.' Well, I can tell you, I got on my knees in my bedroom that day and began confessing my sins to God. There were other people I had to go to and ask for forgiveness too. But, most importantly, I asked God to forgive me and make me clean on the inside, and I have felt different ever since. I still pray from the prayer book sometimes, but now the words mean something and it's the best part of my day. I guess that's what it means when Jesus said that He came so we could have life and have it more abundantly."

"Hi," Matthew gave Elizabeth a hug. "I've missed you this past week."

Elizabeth returned the hug. She loved the way Matthew felt free to say whatever was on his mind.

It was Sunday afternoon and the two had the house to themselves. They sat down at the kitchen table for hot chocolate and some brownies that Elizabeth had made.

"I thought a lot concerning what we talked about last Sunday evening," said Matthew. "I'm not sure exactly what meant when you said you think it takes more than just being Amish? Are you really having second thoughts about joining the baptismal classes?"

Elizabeth was silent several moments before answering. "Why did you get baptized?" she asked.

Matthew looked surprised at her question. "Several reasons I guess. I felt it was the right thing to do. I was nineteen and I wanted to be more serious and settle down."

Elizabeth nodded; she knew that was probably why most of the young people did it. But she wanted to get baptized because the Bible said to be baptized and confess Jesus before man, and because it was a sign that one had found new life and was born again. Maybe now would be the time to tell Matthew how she felt about it all. But what if he didn't understand?

"I want to get baptized," she said at last, not sure how to tell him how she really felt.

"I know you won't be sorry." Matthew squeezed her hand.

Chapter Nineteen

Elizabeth twisted her hands nervously in her lap. Today she was taking her first membership class. For the next several months she and several other young people would gather with the ministers before services, and each of the ministers would give a short speech admonishing them to live right before God according to the Amish faith.

Elizabeth tried to listen carefully as Bishop Joe began speaking. He spoke of beginning a new life, becoming an upbuilding member of the church, and obeying all the rules of their traditions. The class then ended with prayer and everyone joined the rest of the congregation.

"Were you as nervous as I was?" asked Cathy, once services were over.

Elizabeth nodded. "I'm glad I wasn't alone."

Elizabeth liked Cathy Schrock immediately. Her family had just moved into the community from Indiana the week before, and today was the first time they'd met. She was instantly drawn to her sweet friendly personality. As they chatted, Elizabeth thought about a book she'd read where the author had written about kindred spirits. She didn't know if there was such a thing or not, but if there was, then Cathy fit the description. She was looking forward to getting to know her, especially since they were the only girls in the class. Before parting ways that afternoon, the two of them made plans to get together at Elizabeth's house one afternoon that week to work on Elizabeth's quilt.

"Well, how did it go?" asked Matthew that afternoon.

"I was pretty nervous at first," Elizabeth admitted.

"Yes, I remember the feeling," Matthew smiled. "Are you glad you went?"

"I guess so." Elizabeth knew she didn't show much enthusiasm, but Matthew didn't seem to realize.

"I have something I'd like to ask you," said Matthew, changing the subject. "We have never talked about where we will live after we get married, but I was wondering if you would have any objections to moving to our community? I have an opportunity to buy several acres of land close to my parents, but I wanted to ask you first what you thought."

Elizabeth liked hearing the words "when we get married." It sounded so romantic. "I would go anywhere with you," she smiled, adding, "As soon as we are married."

"When is that going to be?" he asked.

"Are you sure you still want to marry me?"

"You are the only girl for me. Surely you know that by now."

Elizabeth nodded. "I never get tired of it hearing it though."

"Then maybe we could think about setting a date," Matthew said seriously.

"I don't know what Dad and Mom will say," Elizabeth hesitated. "I'm only seventeen; I'm afraid they will say I'm too young."

"You'll soon be eighteen though," he reminded her. "We could ask them if we could get married next summer, after your nineteenth birthday."

"I'll have to talk to them and then I'll let you know," Elizabeth answered.

Elizabeth hummed a little tune as she hung the laundry on the line. Matthew wanted to marry her. She felt like the luckiest girl in the world. Now she would just have to find the courage to ask Mom and Dad if they approved.

She thought all forenoon about how she could broach the subject with Mom.

"Mom," she said at last. "Tell me again how old you were when you got married."

Mom smiled to herself, suspecting why Elizabeth was asking. "I was nineteen," she answered.

"And how long did you date?"

"About two years."

Elizabeth took a deep breath. It was now or never. "We...ah...I mean, Matthew and I were wondering if it would be okay with you and Dad if we got married next summer?"

"Are you ready to think about marriage?" asked Mom.

Elizabeth hesitated before answering; she hadn't thought about that before. All she had thought about was being with Matthew every moment of every day.

"What do you mean?" she asked at last.

"Getting married is a big responsibility," said Mom. "It means you are willing to put someone else's happiness before your own."

Elizabeth was silent, thinking about what Mom had said. What were some of the things that made Matthew happy? Were they the same things that made her happy?

"Elizabeth talked to me today," Mom confided to Dad after everyone else had gone to bed.

"About what?" asked Dad, peering over the top of the newspaper.

"She and Matthew would like to get married next summer."

"What did you tell her?"

"I said we would talk it over and let her know," answered Mom.

"Do you have any objections?"

Mom shrugged. "I guess not," she admitted. "It's just that they seem so young to be getting married."

Dad nodded. "Yah, they are, but so were we. Elizabeth's a good girl and Matthew seems like a nice young man. He is in good standing in the church as far as I know, and he has a good job."

Mom smiled. That was just like her husband looking at it from a practical viewpoint. Maybe he was right. She thought back to the struggles she had gone through in the first years of their marriage. She had moved far away from home and had been very lonely, especially before their first baby came. But since Elizabeth wouldn't be so far away, it would be easier for her.

"It just seems hard to believe our youngest child is all grown up and ready for marriage," said Mom, a hint of sadness in her voice. "It just feels like life is passing by too fast."

Dad reached over and took her hand. "We'll just have more grandchildren to enjoy."

Mom nodded. "Yah, I know what ya mean. It's been such a good life though."

"Hi Cathy," Elizabeth greeted her new friend at the door Wednesday afternoon. "I didn't hear you drive in," she said.

"Your brother came and unhitched the horse for me," Cathy replied.

The two girls moved into the living room where the quilt was set up.

"How do you like Pennsylvania by now?" asked Elizabeth.

"I like the all the hills," said Cathy. "Indiana was pretty flat where we lived. But it's all so new yet that it still seems too strange to feel like home."

Elizabeth nodded. "I have lived in Pennsylvania all my life and I can't imagine moving to a strange place."

The girls spent the afternoon getting acquainted. Elizabeth learned that back in Indiana Cathy had worked at a sewing factory. She came from a family of twelve children and she was the fifth child.

"Where do your married brothers and sisters live?" asked Elizabeth.

"They live in Michigan," replied Cathy, "but they aren't Amish anymore."

Elizabeth looked surprised. She couldn't imagine having family that wasn't Amish, knowing the strict shunning practices. Families were separated by it. In some cases they didn't even speak to the ones who left, except to rebuke them. To her it seemed worse than death.

"How did you happen to choose Pennsylvania?" she asked Cathy.

"Dad's brother moved here several years ago and he kept urging my parents to do the same."

"Did you want to come?"

"Yes, I was ready for a new start, a new place," answered Cathy honestly.

Elizabeth smiled. "Well, I'm glad you're here. I hope we can spend a lot of time together." She wondered what Cathy meant by a "new start." Maybe someday when she got to know her better, she would ask her.

Just then Leroy poked his head in the door. "Could you come out earlier tonight to help with the milking?" he asked. "Some of us guys are going fishing."

"What time?" asked Elizabeth, glancing at the clock.

"Maybe around four o'clock. I need you to drop me off at Reeds Four Corners at five o'clock to meet the guys there."

"I could drop you off there on my way home," offered Cathy.

Surprised by her offer, Leroy hesitated, then,. "Sure, why not?" he agreed, and disappeared out the door.

Elizabeth was surprised at how easily Leroy accepted Cathy's offer. He was usually shy around girls and tried to make himself scarce if she or Marilyn had friends over. Most of their friends came sometimes just in hopes of seeing Leroy. But Cathy was different.

Leroy noticed the difference too, when the two girls came out to the barn. She didn't do or say anything to try to get his attention. In fact, she chatted with Elizabeth and seemed to not even notice he was there.

When chores were finished, Leroy hurried to hitch up Cathy's horse. He felt a bit worried. What would he say?

But he needn't have worried. Cathy was no different when they were alone. Her easygoing manner soon had him feeling at ease.

"How do you like Pennsylvania by now?" he asked.

"I like it," said Cathy. "It's kinda like an adventure."

Leroy started to answer, then stopped. There was something lying beside the road in the ditch. "What's that up ahead?" he asked.

Cathy pulled on the reins slowing the horse to a walk. As they got closer, she said, "It looks like a person!"

A moment later they pulled alongside the ditch. Cathy was right. A man was lying there in a crumpled heap.

"It's my dad!" Cathy cried, dropping the reins and jumping out of the buggy.

"What on earth could've happened?" thought Leroy, as he grabbed the reins and tied the horse to a nearby tree. Then, quickly, he grabbed the buggy blanket and hurried over to help Cathy. Between the two of them they soon had her father lying on the blanket.

"Dad," Cathy kept calling softly. "Can you hear me?"

Leroy was puzzled. There were no apparent injuries. How did he get here?

"What shall we do?" cried Cathy, frantically searching for a pulse.

"I'll go call the ambulance," said Leroy running for the road.

Just then a car slowed to a stop. It was Mr. Clayton. It took only a moment for him to see how serious the situation was. "I'll be right back," he threw over his shoulder before he sped off to call for help.

Leroy joined Cathy at her father's side. "Help is on the way," he reassured her.

"Oh, thank you," she said tears rolling down her cheeks. "But what can we do in the meantime?" she cried.

Leroy felt helpless. In an attempt to comfort her he reached over and took her hand. "Help will soon be here," he assured again.

Cathy clung to his hand. It seemed like an eternity passed by as they sat and waited before hearing the first sounds of a siren off in the distance.

Leroy sighed with relief when the ambulance arrived. There was a flurry of activity as the medical professionals jumped from the ambulance and swooped down on Mr. Schrock.

In a matter of minutes they had him loaded on a stretcher, all the while working frantically in an attempt to get a heartbeat.

As they prepared to leave, Leroy turned to Cathy. "You go with the ambulance and I'll go let your Mom know."

After giving Leroy directions, Cathy was ushered into the ambulance and whisked away to the hospital with her father.

Just then Mr. Clayton returned, offering his services. Sending him to the Schrock farm, Leroy untied the horse and made his way there as well. It felt good to be doing something. He had felt so helpless waiting for the ambulance. The evening had sure turned out much different than he planned.

Leroy pulled on the reins guiding the horse into the Schrock's lane where Mr. Clayton had filled Cathy's mother in on what little he knew of the incident. "I'll take you to the hospital," he offered.

"Could you stay here with the boys?" she asked Leroy.

Assuring her that he would gladly stay until she returned, Leroy drove up to the barn and unhitched the horse, then he made his way to the house. It was a huge old farmhouse with a wraparound porch. A porch swing and several rockers gave it a homey feel, resembling something out of a magazine. Several huge maple trees around the house made the picture complete.

Leroy knocked on the door.

Soon a boy of about seven or eight answered the door. Leroy hesitated before stepping inside. Was this the only child here? Just then several more little boys appeared.

Leroy introduced himself and said their mother had asked him to stay until she returned.

The biggest of the boys seemed relieved. "Do you think Dad will be okay?" he asked anxiously.

Leroy didn't know what to answer. It certainly hadn't looked good, he thought, remembering the unconscious form that had been placed in the ambulance and rushed to the hospital.

"We won't know until they get back." He chose his words carefully.

"Where was your dad going today?" he asked, hoping to shed some light on the mystery.

"He rode horseback over to Uncle Raymond's this afternoon," answered the oldest boy, whom Leroy learned was named Andy.

Understanding dawned on Leroy. He must've fallen off his horse. Maybe he'd had a heart attack. He remembered hearing the words "cardiac arrest" when the paramedics were working on Mr. Schrock at the scene.

"Where's the horse now?" asked Leroy.

"I don't know," shrugged Andy.

"Shall we go see if he's out by the barn?"

The boys eagerly followed Leroy. Sure enough, there, behind the barn, was the horse, saddle and bridle still intact.

Andy caught the horse easily and put him into the barn.

Leroy glanced at the other little boys and did a quick headcount. There were five of them, ranging in ages from fifteen to two, he guessed.

"Have you had supper?" he asked, as they headed back to the house.

The boys shook their heads. "I'm hungry," said the littlest boy named Ivan.

"I can make something for you," said Leroy, picking him up and carrying him the rest of the way.

Leroy was glad for something to do to pass the time. He rummaged through the cupboards and refrigerator until he found all the ingredients to make an omelet which he served along with chocolate milk.

The boys soon lost their shyness and offered to help. Leroy tried to remember all their names. Andy was the oldest, then there was Eli, Vern, Amos and Ivan. He enjoyed watching the way they all seemed anxious to help—setting the table and bringing chairs.

"Can you tell me a story?" asked Ivan, crawling up into Leroy's lap after supper while the rest of the boys cleared the table.

"Oh, don't bother him," said Eli.

"That's okay," said Leroy, settling back in the rocking chair. The poor little guy looked tired, and he had somehow won his way into Leroy's soft heart.

Before the first story was over, Ivan had fallen fast asleep in Leroy's arms. He laid the book aside wondering what to do with the little guy. But he didn't have to decide as just then the door opened and Cathy entered the living room her mother behind her.

Leroy didn't need to hear the words to know. Their grief-stricken faces told him that Mr. Schrock was gone. His heart ached as he watched the family cling together, sobbing.

"Thank you for everything." Cathy left her other brothers to take Ivan from Leroy's arms.

"Is there anything else I can do?" asked Leroy.

"No…yes, just hang on a minute." Cathy left the room and came back with a list of phone numbers. "Could you call these numbers and tell them?"

Leroy nodded. Taking the list and promising Andy to be back in the morning to help with the chores, he headed out the door.

Elizabeth's heart ached for Cathy and her family.

"What will they do?" she asked Leroy several days later, when they were on their way home from helping with the chores at the Schrock's.

Leroy shrugged. "I don't know how they'll manage," he said. "Andy is only fifteen and he's the oldest boy at home. They will need a lot of help with the farm this summer."

Elizabeth agreed. "I don't know what Mrs. Schrock would do without Cathy," she said.

"Yes," Leroy replied. "She seems so strong and takes care of those little boys." He shook his head. "She's quite something."

"She reminds me a lot of Rachel," said Elizabeth quietly. "I feel like I could get close to her like I was to Rachel. She's so sweet."

"You still miss Rachel a lot, don't you?" Leroy asked.

"Yes I do. The horrible ache is gone now, but I miss not having a best friend to tell girl stuff to."

"Won't Matt listen to all that girl stuff?"

Elizabeth laughed. "I don't know that any guy is willing to do that!"

"Maybe not, but if I ever have a girlfriend, I want her to be my best friend too, and for us to be able to tell each other all our dreams."

"That sound very romantic," Elizabeth teased. "Do you have anyone in mind?"

"No, can't say as I do."

"You're twenty-three years old," said Elizabeth. "Aren't you ready to think of getting married?"

"Maybe, if the right girl comes along," her brother admitted. "But you are married longer than you are single in life, so what's the rush?"

Elizabeth laughed at Leroy's analogy. "I've never thought of it that way before, but I reckon you're right."

Chapter Twenty

In the weeks following Mr. Schrock's death, Leroy and Elizabeth found themselves spending more and more time at the Schrock home—either to help with the chores or just going to visit.

"I don't know what we'd do without Leroy's help," commented Cathy on one such occasion as she and Elizabeth relaxed on the porch swing. "I don't know how we'll ever pay you two back for all your help."

"Don't feel like that! We enjoy spending time with your family, and Leroy likes your little brothers."

"Not many guys would do it without expecting something," commented Cathy.

Elizabeth looked questioningly at Cathy, waiting for her to explain.

Cathy sighed. "Two weeks ago Calvin Bontreger came over to help plant the corn. When he was ready to leave, I thanked him for helping, so then he took the opportunity to ask me out on a date."

"You've got to be kidding!" said Elizabeth disgustedly.

Cathy shook her head and continued. "He made me feel obligated, but I could never lower my standards just so someone will help us. Needless to say he hasn't been back since," she finished.

Elizabeth knew almost every boy in the community had their eyes on Cathy. She was very pretty with her big blue eyes, blonde hair, and slim figure.

"How's your mom doing?" asked Elizabeth, changing the subject.

"She gets so lonely," said Cathy. "I feel so bad for her. She told me the other day it feels constantly as if something is missing. Every morning it feels like it just happened, and it takes an effort just to get out of bed and face the day."

"How long were they married?" asked Elizabeth.

"Twenty-seven years," answered Cathy. "She says one of the hardest things is knowing that little Ivan won't remember him."

Elizabeth nodded. She couldn't even begin to imagine what the family was going through.

She knew Cathy bore a huge part of the responsibility, looking after the chores and helping take care of her little brothers. "Leroy said your brother from Michigan was thinking of moving here to help out," she said.

Cathy sighed. "He would like to, but I don't think the church here will allow it. He was never a member of the Amish church but Bishop Joe told Mom it could cause problems. So I don't think he will, although it would be so nice to have his help."

"I know people around here are very strict in their shunning practices," Elizabeth said slowly.

The conversation ended just then when Leroy and Andy joined them on the porch.

"Leroy says the hay looks like it's ready to mow," stated Andy.

"I haven't a clue what to do," said Cathy looking at Leroy, "but if you'll tell us what to do maybe we can get it ourselves."

"I'll help," Leroy offered.

"You've done way more than your share already," Cathy protested. "I hope someday we can repay you."

Leroy smiled. "Ah, don't worry about it. What are neighbors for?" As he and Elizabeth made their way out to the buggy, he called back over his shoulder, "I'll be by around nine tomorrow morning."

"Well, tell me, what's the latest gossip?" teased Leroy, once they were headed for home.

"What makes you ask that?" said Elizabeth defensively.

"Oh come on!" he laughed. "I can see it in your face that you know something, your stewin' and brewin' about."

Elizabeth grinned in spite of herself, knowing she'd been busted. "Okay, since you think you're so smart I'll tell you," she said, telling him what Cathy had told her earlier that evening about guys offering to help, and then asking her out.

Leroy shook his head in disgust. He had heard some of the talk going around about Cathy's looks and figure, but had never joined in. He felt those kinds of remarks were disrespectful and crude. "I know the other week when we had a service there, she was setting food on the table at lunchtime and some of the guys were trying to flirt with her, but she just gave them the brush off very gracefully."

"That's Cathy, all right," said Elizabeth admiringly. "She's too good for any of those guys."

"I suppose you know who would be her perfect mate," Leroy said mockingly.

"As a matter of fact, I do have someone in mind." Elizabeth looked at her brother very pointedly.

Leroy shook his head. "You're a hopeless case," he said laughing.

The next morning dawned bright and clear. A heavy dew had fallen the night before, and the blades of grass glistened in the sun like millions of little diamonds. Leroy loved a cool clear morning like this. "It's a perfect day for mowing," he thought, as he rode over to the Schrock's farm.

Two of the younger boys ran out to meet Leroy and both spoke at the same time, "Andy broke his arm!"

"Oh, no!" said Leroy sympathetically. "What happened?"

"He fell out of the haymow," said the younger of the two feeling very important to be able to share this information with Leroy. Mom took him to the doctor."

"I guess you've already heard the news," said Cathy coming around the corner of the barn.

"Yes, that's too bad," Leroy said. "Is he going to be okay?"

Cathy nodded. "I'm going to try and help in his place," she said. "But I'll have to warn you, I've never done this before."

"Mostly it's just driving the horses," explained Leroy, "and knowing how to turn and pull up the mower blades at the ends of the fields."

"Sounds easy for you," Cathy said, "but I'm not very good at all this farming stuff. Dad and my brothers always did it."

After harnessing up the horses the two of them headed for the hay field.

The first several rounds were anything but easy. Cathy had a hard time remembering Leroy's instructions. "I'm afraid I'm making more work than anything," she despaired.

"No, you're doing fine," encouraged Leroy.

Cathy shook her head, feeling tears close to the surface. "You're just being nice," she said.

Several rounds later, however, she had finally gotten the hang of it and was ready to try it on her own.

Leroy stood back and watched her struggle to pull on the lever that pulled up the mower blade, smiling at her determination. Seeing that she was able to do it this time without any assistance, he began cutting hay with the second mower, humming to himself as he went. He loved the smell of the freshly cut hay and, he realized as he worked, he also enjoyed Cathy's company. There was something different about her, something special. The way she looked after her mother and her little brothers, it was more than any girl her age should have to do.

"Want some lemonade, Leroy?" called Vern, breaking into Leroy's musings.

Leroy nodded, pulling the horses to a halt. "This sure hits the spot," he smiled at the little boy. "Did you make it?"

Vern nodded proudly. "I made Cathy some too."

"That's nice," Leroy said, hopping back on the mower. "Thank you."

The rest of the forenoon passed uneventfully and by lunchtime the mowing was almost finished.

"I can get the rest after lunch if you want to head home," Cathy said at the dining room table. "We've already taken up so much of your time."

"You worry too much," said Leroy. "What are friends for?"

"Maybe you're right, but I do want you to know how much I appreciate your help."

"You're welcome." Leroy gave her a big smile before riding away.

"That's too bad," said Elizabeth after hearing of Andy's misfortune. "Who helped you with the mowing then?"

"Cathy," answered Leroy, sitting down beside the cow to began the milking.

Elizabeth glanced at Marilyn. "Did you hear that?"

Marilyn grinned. "So it was just the two of you all by yourselves way back in the hayfield? she asked. "Sounds pretty romantic to me."

Leroy kept his face hidden behind the cow so the girls wouldn't see his face. He had enjoyed the day very much and suddenly realized he was looking forward to the next time he would have an excuse to go over to the Schrock farm.

Chapter Twenty-One

"This summer is going by too fast for me," declared Elizabeth as she and Cathy settled down beneath the shade tree. "I have been so busy these past two weeks, first Nelson and Linda had a baby girl, and then a couple days later Daniel and Anna had a little boy. That makes twelve nieces and nephews for me."

"You are lucky you get to enjoy them," said Cathy wistfully. "I hardly ever get to see my brothers' and sisters' children."

"I guess I just take my family for granted too much," Elizabeth replied sympathetically.

"Do you have your baptismal dress made?" Cathy asked.

"You mean the 'traditional black dress'?" Elizabeth made up a face, then answered Cathy's question. "Yes, I finally finished it yesterday. I'm not too fond of sewing."

"I enjoy sewing," said Cathy. "I'd much rather sew than work outside."

Elizabeth laughed. She knew working outside had been a trial to Cathy. "This has been a hard summer for you, hasn't it?"

Cathy nodded. "But I've learned a lot, and got the best tan I've ever had."

"Do you ever have second thoughts about becoming a member of the Amish church?" asked Elizabeth, changing the subject.

Cathy didn't answer for several moments. "Why do you ask?"

"Well," answered Elizabeth, "it's just that after next Sunday you'll have to shun your brothers and sisters."

Cathy's eyes filled with tears. "I've thought about that."

The girls sat in silence for several moments.

"What does baptism mean to you?" Elizabeth asked, finally breaking the silence.

"Several things, I guess. One is that I will be a member of the Amish church, and it washes away our sins."

Elizabeth nodded. "I used to wish that I could die the day I get baptized so that I could know for sure that I was going to heaven."

"I know exactly what you mean," agreed Cathy.

"But I don't feel like that anymore." Elizabeth took a deep breath praying silently that God would help her to let Cathy know how much He loved her. "I know now that it's the blood of Jesus that washes away my sins. Baptism is only an outward sign that Jesus already washed away my sins."

"I wish I felt that way," said Cathy longingly. "But there are things you don't know about me. I've done some bad things and I knew better before I did them; I mean, I knew it was sin. Can God really forgive us for things when we knew better than to do them?"

"Could you carry Chris out to the van for me?" Anna asked, looking at Matthew.

"Sure," he smiled, setting his nephew up on his shoulder and heading for the door. Then he called over his shoulder, "Would you let me know how Elizabeth's doing?"

Anna stopped short. "Matthew, you never told me that you were interested!"

Matthew smiled sheepishly. "I tried to tell her once," he confessed, "but we were interrupted so I don't know how she feels," he said.

"Are you serious?" questioned Anna bluntly.

Matthew shrugged. "I know I've liked her for a long time," he admitted.

"Then you had better make sure you are serious before you let her know. Don't break her heart. She's a sweet girl, and she's been through enough."

Matthew nodded. "You're right," he agreed. "I'll have to do some serious thinking on it."

Chapter Thirteen

It wasn't until two days later that Elizabeth woke up again.

"Mom," she whispered, "is that you?"

"Yes it's me," said Mom squeezing Elizabeth's hand and feeling overcome with joy.

"Where am I?" Elizabeth asked.

"You're in the hospital," her mom told her. "But don't worry; everything is okay."

"Is Dad here too?"

"Yes, I'm right here," her dad said. "You just rest."

"My head hurts," Elizabeth groaned.

"I'll get the nurse and see what she can do for you." Dad left the room and went in search of the nurse.

"How long have I been here?" Elizabeth asked several days later when she was able to stay awake for awhile.

"I think it's six days now," said Dena.

"What happened?" Elizabeth asked.

"Don't you remember?" Dena waited tensely for Elizabeth to respond. The doctor had warned them that she could suffer a short-term memory loss.

Elizabeth tried to think back. It seemed like such a long time ago. Everything was fuzzy. She was on her way somewhere...Oh yes, now she remembered. She was driving Champ!

"Champ ran away," she said slowly, trying to recall exactly what had happened.

"Why did he run away?" Dena asked.

"It was the deer," said Elizabeth. "Two deer jumped out in front of us and scared Champ. Is Leroy upset that Champ ran away?" she asked.

Dena shook her head, relieved that Elizabeth hadn't thought to ask what happened to Champ. There would be plenty of time to deal with that later.

"I could've gotten killed," said Elizabeth realizing the seriousness of her accident.

Dena agreed. "It sure gave us all a scare."

"A year ago I wouldn't have been ready to die," said Elizabeth, staring at the ceiling.

"Are you ready now?" asked Dena, trying to understand what Elizabeth meant.

Elizabeth nodded. "I used to always be afraid to die because I thought I couldn't know if I was going to heaven or if God could forgive my sins." She went on to tell Dena about the passages Rachel had shown her from the Bible. "I can't tell you how much different I feel than I used to. Jesus is real to me now."

Dena wiped her tears as she listened to Elizabeth. She felt hungry to experience the peace her sister was talking about. She had seen a change in Elizabeth over the past year, definitely something special. Now she knew what it was.

"I don't know if you're ready to ask Jesus to come into your heart today and give you a new life," Elizabeth looked at Dena, "but He died to wash away your sins—not just the sins of the past but the sins of the future too. That's why we need to ask Him in our daily prayers to forgive us our trespasses like it says in the Lord's Prayer."

Dena nodded. "I guess I would like to go home and read those verses," she said at last.

Elizabeth pressed on. "Just remember in Deuteronomy 4:29 it says, 'Seek the Lord your God and you will find Him if you seek Him with all your heart.'"

"I have never been so glad to be home in my life!" Elizabeth exclaimed happily, looking around at everything that was dear and familiar. The hickory rockers, the braided rugs, the old-fashioned oil lamps, even the way the house smelled of Mom's homemade soap.

"We're glad you're home too, squirt," said Leroy.

"I'd be careful what I say if I was you," warned Elizabeth. "These crutches may reach farther than you think."

Leroy laughed heartily. "I'm glad you didn't lose your spunk."

"I may have taken a bump on the head," Elizabeth laughed too, "but I can still beat you at checkers."

"Talk is cheap," said Leroy. "Let's just wait and see."

Elizabeth felt overwhelmed at all the attention she received in the weeks following her accident. Marilyn's pupils made her get-well cards, and every family in the community dropped by for a visit, bringing gifts. There were water sets, dishes, towels, beautiful handmade pillows, blankets, afghans, and books. And before long the beautiful hope chest Leroy had made her was overflowing. Elizabeth was deeply touched by everyone's kindness.

"Oh Mom," she said one day, "I feel so unworthy of all this."

"Yah, I know what you mean," agreed Mom. "The church took up a collection on Sunday and it was enough to pay the hospital bill."

Grateful, Elizabeth hoped she would someday be able to pass on all the kindness shown her.

"More mail for you," said Mom later that day, handing Elizabeth a stack of cards and letters.

"Another letter from Grandma, one from Aunt Millie, oh and here's one from Nancy," said Elizabeth, tearing open the envelope. "She says some of the 'youngie' from there plan to come here Friday night."

"That's nice." Mom responded. "Are they coming for supper?"

"No, after supper," said Elizabeth, "but maybe we could serve fruit pizza for a snack."

"I think that could be arranged." Mom was glad to see how much Nancy's letter had cheered Elizabeth up. She knew her daughter was getting tired of sitting in the house day after day.

"Do you think I could wear a dress tonight?" asked Elizabeth on Friday afternoon.

"How are you going to get your cast through the sleeve of your dress?" asked Marilyn.

Elizabeth shrugged. "I don't know, but I'm sick of wearing of nightgowns and robes all the time."

Marilyn laughed. She knew Elizabeth was tired of needing everyone's help. But with a cast on her leg and one on her arm, it was no easy task to get dressed without help.

Attired in her pink nightgown and white robe, Elizabeth relaxed in the recliner to read until her guests arrived. For a brief moment she wondered if Matthew might be among those coming to visit her this evening. "Don't be silly," she said to herself. "He has better things to do than visit an invalid." With that thought in mind, she opened her book and began reading.

"Your company is here," Mom announced from the kitchen sometime later. "I'll bring them into the living room, so don't try to get up." She knew Elizabeth's ribs were still sore.

"Hi," smiled Nancy, coming into the living room ahead of everyone else. "Are you ready for company?"

"Do I have a choice?" Elizabeth teased. "I can't very well run away, can I?"

"I see you haven't lost your sense of humor," Nancy laughed. "How are you feeling?"

"Much better," said Elizabeth, "although I can hardly wait for these casts to come off."

Soon several more young people joined them in the living room. Elizabeth felt her heart beat a little faster when she looked up to see Matthew come across the room to greet her.

"Hi," he smiled, looking down at her nestled among the pillows on the recliner. He was sure he had never seen her look sweeter. "How are you doing?" he asked.

Elizabeth smiled back. "Pretty good," she said, unable to take her eyes off his. There was something different about him. He looked taller, she thought, and definitely cuter than she had remembered.

"When will your casts come off?" he asked.

"A couple more weeks."

Their conversation was interrupted when several more people joined them and began asking questions of their own.

Elizabeth enjoyed the evening. The boys played ping-pong, while the girls watched and cheered them on. All too soon the evening was over and everyone got ready to leave, wishing Elizabeth well, and thanking her mother for the treats.

Elizabeth sighed contentedly as she snuggled under the covers, thinking about what Nancy had whispered in her ear before she left. "I just thought you'd like to know that Matthew asked Eugene if he could come along tonight."

Elizabeth felt a warm fuzzy feeling close to her heart every time she thought about that smile and those mischievous blue eyes.

The long awaited day finally arrived. The casts were coming off!

"It feels so good to be back to normal," sighed Elizabeth happily. "I'll even be glad to help Leroy milk."

"Remember what the doctor said though," reminded Mom. "Be careful not to overdo it."

Elizabeth laughed. "Oh Mom, you worry too much. I'm good as new again."

Chapter Fourteen

Matthew opened his desk and took out a tablet and pen. He had done some serious thinking about what Anna had said to him about Elizabeth and had decided to write her a letter. But what would he say? He certainly didn't want to hurt her. Putting his pen to the paper he wrote, "Dear Elizabeth," then he stopped. Maybe he should pray first, but how? He was accustomed to reciting prayers from the prayer book. Certainly if he was serious he should ask God if Elizabeth was the one.

Matthew laid his pen down and walked over to the window. The hills were just beginning to turn green and everything had fresh new life. He loved the spring of the year. He opened the window; maybe the fresh air would clear his head. Would Elizabeth even say yes?

Matthew thought about the evening he spent at her house a month ago. Did she feel the same way he did or was it just wishful thinking? He thought also about the time they'd shared that sweet little kiss. Surely she felt the same way. Well, there was only one way to find out. He would write and ask her. He went back to his desk and started writing again.

Dear Elizabeth,
How are you? Are your casts off yet?
I have been thinking about you a lot lately. I have never written a letter like this before so I'm not sure what to say. I would like to get to know you better. I would like to come spend next Sunday afternoon with you. If you feel the same, please let me know.
Sincerely,
Matthew

Sighing with relief, Matthew folded the letter and got it ready to mail. Now all he had to do was wait for Elizabeth's answer.

"Oh good, there's the mailman." Elizabeth shut off the lawnmower. "I need a break." Opening the mailbox, she drew out a stack of mail and headed for porch swing where she glanced through the stack of envelopes. "Probably just junk mail," she said aloud. "Nope, here's one for me with no return address." Stuffing the letter in her pocket she decided to wait until she was in the privacy of her room to read it. The handwriting was definitely a guy's handwriting, she thought, but whose?

"Here's the mail," she called to Mom, throwing it on the kitchen table.

To curious to wait any longer to see who her letter was from, she ran up the stairs to her room and quickly tore open the envelope. Her eyes darted to the bottom of the page to see who it was from. Matthew! Elizabeth's heart beat a little faster. Sitting down on the edge of the bed she read it slowly, taking in each word. She had gotten letters like this before but this was different. Should she say yes? She knew she liked Matthew, but was he the one she wanted to date—and maybe marry?

These thoughts were still going through her mind when she went out to do the chores that evening. How did she know if he was the right one? He only asked for one date, she scolded herself, not marriage. But in her heart she knew she should pray and ask God to help her make the right decision.

The next evening Elizabeth settled down on the sofa in her room with pen and paper in hand. She had given Matthew's letter a lot of thought the past two days; in fact, it was practically all she had thought about. Now was the hard part. What should she write? She had never written to a boy before.

Dear Matthew,
Thank you for your letter. My casts are off, and I am glad to be back to normal.
Yes, I would like it if you came to see me on Sunday.
Elizabeth

Elizabeth read and reread the letter several times before mailing it. She, Elizabeth Hostetler, was going to have her first date next Sunday.

"Do you want to go along to the gathering this afternoon?" asked Marilyn, poking her head into Elizabeth's room.

"No, I think I'll just stay home," answered Elizabeth, hoping Marilyn wouldn't ask why. She hadn't told anyone Matthew was coming for their first date.

"Okay, well then, I guess we're off." Marilyn ran down the stairs to catch Leroy.

"Isn't Elizabeth coming?" he asked.

Marilyn smiled, "No, she said she thinks she'll just stay home, but I think there's something else going on."

Leroy looked puzzled. "Is someone coming to see her?" he asked.

"I think so," said Marilyn. "She's been acting strange all week."

Elizabeth glanced through the dresses in her closet for the fiftieth time. "What color should I wear?" she asked herself. Finally she settled on her light blue knit dress.

"Elizabeth," Mom called upstairs. "Dad and I are going for a walk. We won't be gone long."

"Okay," Elizabeth called back, relieved that no one would be home. She hadn't told anyone that Matthew was coming to see her. Traditionally, Amish youth had their dates on Sunday evenings. After the hymn singing the boy would take the girl to her home where they would either sit at the kitchen table or on the living room sofa. Elizabeth knew some girls were allowed to take their dates up to their bedrooms but she knew her parents would not permit that.

Ever so carefully Elizabeth got dressed, making sure everything was neatly pinned in place. She glanced at the clock—it was two o'clock. Mathew hadn't said what time he was coming, so she decided to head downstairs and wait. Sitting in her favorite rocker, she picked up a magazine and began flipping through it. Just then she heard a knock. Suddenly feeling very nervous, she hurried to the door.

"Hi," she smiled. "Come in."

"Hi," Matthew smiled back, stepping inside. A nervous silence followed as the two of them stood there, both wondering what to say next.

Finally Matthew spoke, "I…uh…this is kinda new to me. I hope I don't make a mess of it."

Elizabeth felt relieved. "I know what you mean," she smiled. "I feel the same way."

"Where's everyone at?" Matthew looked around.

"Leroy and Marilyn went to the youth gathering and Dad and Mom walked over to the neighbors."

"Did they know I was coming?" Matthew asked.

Elizabeth shook her head. "I didn't tell anyone."

Matthew grinned. "Neither did I."

The afternoon passed by quickly as the two got acquainted. They laughed and talked while sitting on the porch swing enjoying popcorn and lemonade.

"Shall we go for a walk?" asked Matthew, getting up to stretch his legs.

"Sure," Elizabeth agreed.

Matthew reached over and took Elizabeth's hand. "Do you know how long I've waited for this day?" he asked as they walked along.

Blushing Elizabeth shrugged. "I don't know."

"I was going to ask you that day at the supermarket, but Nancy interrupted me."

They continued on in silence for several moments.

"Could I come see you again next Sunday?" Matthew asked when they were back at the house.

"Yes, that would be nice," Elizabeth told him. "I enjoyed today very much."

"So did I," said Matthew, squeezing her hand. "But I should get going." He looked at his watch. "May I kiss you before I go?" he asked hesitantly.

Elizabeth nodded shyly.

Holding her close Matthew brushed his lips softly against hers. "I'll see you next Sunday," he said.

Elizabeth watched by the window until Matthew drove down the lane and out of sight, then she climbed the stairs to her room, feeling as if her feet were hardly touching the ground. Closing the door to her room, she lit the lamp and sat down on the edge of the bed. She thought back over the day remembering all the things they'd talked about. She liked the way he smiled and his mischievous blue eyes. And, best of all, he wanted to come see her again next Sunday.

"Was it just my imagination or were you smiling at the cow today?" Leroy teased, when they finished with the milking Monday morning.

"I'm going to ignore your teasing," said Elizabeth, turning her back to him.

"Aw come on," said Leroy. "That's no fun."

"Maybe you should ask Leroy why he's so happy?" Marilyn spoke up.

"Come on, tell me," Elizabeth begged.

"First you tell me who your date was last night?" Leroy bargained.

"What makes you think I had a date?" asked Elizabeth.

"I know that you did," he answered, "and I'll guess that it was Matthew Yoder."

"Why would you say that?" she asked curiously.

"I'm not blind," said Leroy laughing. "He's had a crush on you since you were fifteen."

"Okay," Elizabeth she admitted grudgingly," she said, "so tell me what's your big news? You'd better tell me if you want my help with the chores again to night!"

"Okay, I'll tell you. Betty Kiem asked me to be her partner at her sister's wedding next week." He grinned.

"What shall we make for your birthday supper tomorrow night?" Mom asked Elizabeth.

"How about lasagna?" said Elizabeth. "That's my favorite."

"Anything else? We'll make whatever you like."

"Well," Elizabeth thought a minute, "I'd rather have rhubarb pie than cake."

"The married ones are all coming tomorrow night too, so maybe we can have both," Mom told Elizabeth. She watched as her daughter headed out to the garden.

Where have these past seventeen years gone? she asked herself. It seemed like such a short time ago that she was just a toddler in her lap, and now here she was a young lady, with a beau! She knew Elizabeth and Matthew had been dating for the last two months. Not that she disapproved of the relationship, Matthew was twenty, so she supposed he was serious. At least, she hoped so. She would hate to see Elizabeth get her heart broken. She knew Elizabeth had certainly grown up a lot this past year with all she had been through, but her heart ached for her as only a mother's can, knowing that life for her had really only just begun and there would inevitably be more hurt and disappointments. She just prayed that God would keep His hand upon her and lead her in the narrow way.

"I heard a van drive in," said Mom to Elizabeth. "I suppose it's Nelson and Linda."

Nelson and Linda now lived thirty-five miles away, too far to drive with horse and buggy, so each time when they came home, they hired an Amish taxi driver to bring them.

Elizabeth looked out the window, "Yes it's them, I'll go get the twins," she offered, setting the plates on the table. Approaching the van, she stopped in surprise. "Matthew!" she exclaimed. "I didn't know you were coming along tonight."

Matthew grinned, enjoying her surprise.

"You weren't supposed to know," laughed Linda.

Matthew liked watching Elizabeth with her little nieces and nephews. He liked the way she listened to every little thing they said. Even though they had only dated for two months, as he watched her carry baby Jonathan out to the kitchen, he knew at that moment that he wanted someday for it to be *their* baby Elizabeth was carrying. The thought surprised him. He had never even thought of himself as getting married and having children before. But with Elizabeth, well, she was special.

Supper was soon over and Elizabeth was excused from the dishes to spend time with Matthew.

"Shall we go sit on the porch swing?" Elizabeth suggested.

"You go ahead, I'll be there in a minute," he said.

Elizabeth headed out to the swing, wondering what Matthew had up his sleeve. She didn't have long to wait, as he soon appeared with a neatly wrapped package.

Opening it, she gasped with delight as she saw a pretty hand-painted oil lamp and matching shade. "It's pink!" she exclaimed. "How did you know I like pink?"

"I asked Anna," he grinned sheepishly.

"Thank you. I've always wanted one of these."

Matthew then surprised her again.

"There's something I would like to ask you," he said, reaching over to take her hand. "I know we've been together every weekend now since our first date, but just to make it official, I'd like to ask you to go steady." By her pleased smile, Matthew knew what her answer would be even before she said yes.

"Do you know when I first started liking you?" he asked.

Elizabeth shook her head.

"The first time I remember seeing you was at Daniel's birthday supper," said Matthew.

"Same here," agreed Elizabeth. "I told Rachel I thought you were cute, but I also told her I thought you were wicked for winking at me."

"I remember the look you gave me," Matthew chuckled. "But I think it was the day I hurt your arm that I started really noticing you."

Elizabeth nodded. "Me too, but then that day I let you kiss me, I was afraid you thought I let all the guys kiss me."

Matthew shook his head, "No, I didn't think that," he reassured her. "But maybe you thought that about me?"

They both laughed at the memory.

"I've got some news to tell you," said Matthew, changing the subject. "I met Nancy and Eugene in town today. They are getting married next month."

"Nancy just turned seventeen in January," said Elizabeth surprised.

Matthew was quiet a moment, wondering how to put it delicately. "They have to get married," he said finally.

"Oh Matthew," Elizabeth's voice was sad. "You know how people will talk. I feel sorry for them, even though I know they did wrong."

"Yes, I know," Matthew agreed. "I find it hard to understand this whole thing of shunning someone after they've confessed and repented."

Elizabeth nodded in agreement. She felt the same way.

Elizabeth lit the lamp beside the bed and sat down. It was hard to believe she was seventeen already. So much had happened this past year. She'd lost her friend Rachel, then she had the accident, and now she had a boyfriend. She thought about what Matthew told her about Nancy and Eugene. She knew of no greater shame among their people than when a young girl became pregnant out of wedlock. Now Nancy wouldn't be allowed to have the traditional big wedding every girl dreams of. Elizabeth knew she must be heartbroken.

"Oh Lord," she prayed, "help me to keep myself pure."

Picking up her Bible, Elizabeth opened it to the front page and read again the words Rachel had written one year ago. Her eyes brimmed with tears as she remembered their conversation that day. "God really loves us," she had told Elizabeth.

Elizabeth knew that was true, but she had trouble feeling it in her heart sometimes. But not Rachel! "That's how I go on every day," she had said. "God didn't give me this cancer; God would never give His children sickness, just like our parents would never give us sickness." Elizabeth had nodded finding it hard to grasp it all.

"Ever since I could remember I dreamed of having a boyfriend and getting married," Rachel had continued on. "But then I got cancer and everything changed. One day I knew I would never live to fulfill my dreams. Then I met Jesus, and I found out that even if I would've lived to have all my dreams come true, I still wouldn't have been satisfied. Because I know now Jesus is the only thing that can truly make you happy and satisfied."

Elizabeth felt overwhelmed with loneliness for Rachel. How she wished she were here to pray with her. Rachel was the only one she could tell her most personal thoughts to. I wonder if I'll ever be able to tell Matthew how I feel, she thought. "Oh Lord," she prayed, "please be with me in this coming year. Be the center of my life. Lead me and guide me in the path you have for me. Help me not to stray from it. In Jesus' name I pray, Amen."

Chapter Fifteen

"It's a year now that Rachel passed away, isn't it?" asked Mom, as she and Elizabeth worked together husking sweet corn.

"Yes, a year ago today was her funeral," replied Elizabeth. "She told me she wouldn't live to see sixteen, and she was right. She died two days before her sixteenth birthday."

"I was thinking you should go and visit her family," said Mom. "You haven't been there since the funeral, have you?"

Elizabeth shook her head. "But Mom, I don't know if I could do it. It'd be so hard, it would bring back so many memories of Rachel."

Mom nodded her head in agreement. "I know, but I think they would like to see you again. You spent a lot of time there last year. It would do you, and them, both some good. I know it's been hard for you to go on without Rachel, but I think this might help you get some closure too."

"I suppose you're right," Elizabeth agreed, seeing the wisdom of her mother's words. "When shall I go?"

"How about tomorrow afternoon?" suggested Mom.

And so the following afternoon Elizabeth found herself on her way to the Yoder's. Her heart felt heavy with emotion as she reflected back over past trips made to that house.

"Elizabeth!" Mrs. Yoder greeted her at the door, sounding both pleased and surprised. "What brings you by?"

Elizabeth was silent for several moments trying to swallow the lump in her throat. She looked around the living room. Everything was so dearly familiar that she almost expected to see Rachel appear. She tried to choke back her tears.

Mrs. Yoder reached over and laid her hand on Elizabeth's arm. "I know there are times when I just expect to see her come into a room, or to be sitting at her place at the table." She paused to wipe away the tears.

"I'm sorry I didn't come before," Elizabeth sobbed.

"That's okay," said Mrs. Yoder. "Would you like some lemonade?"

Elizabeth nodded and followed her into the kitchen. The two sat down at the table.

"Doris, Esther, we have company," called Mrs. Yoder. "Could you make some lemonade?"

Moments later Rachel's two younger sisters appeared with a tray of cookies and several tall glasses of lemonade.

Elizabeth stared in disbelief at the two. "My, you have grown so tall!" she exclaimed.

"Yes, they have," Mrs. Yoder smiled at the girls. "They have grown up too. They are such a help to me. I don't know what I'd do without them."

The four of them spent the next two hours talking about Rachel, reliving fond memories. Sometimes laughing, sometimes shedding a tear.

Finally Elizabeth pushed her chair away from the table. "I suppose I'd best get going," she said regretfully. "But it has been so good to see you all again."

"Yah, it has done us good too," said Mrs. Yoder. "It helps to talk about her with someone who loved her as much as we did."

Elizabeth felt like singing on her way home. She thought about how Mrs. Yoder talked about the great love Rachel had for her Savior. She wanted everyone in her family to pray the prayer of salvation with her. Her love for Jesus was her life. What He had done for her on the cross had become real to her. It was not just a story anymore. She wanted everyone she knew to know that God loved them. And Elizabeth was glad, because she knew Rachel's love for Jesus had touched her life too.

Chapter Sixteen

"Elizabeth," Leroy called. "Where's my target?"

"Your what?"

"My target," he repeated. "I hope you didn't throw it away on one of your cleaning sprees."

"Oh no, don't tell me its that time of the year again." Elizabeth groaned.

"Well, you'd better get used to it," said Leroy. "Matthew likes deer hunting too. He's going to Colorado this fall to hunt, right?"

Elizabeth nodded. "I know," she said handing him his target. "I just don't see what's so exciting about deer hunting anyhow, I mean, really, how hard can it be to walk back in the woods and shoot a deer?"

"Well, I'd would like to see you try it," Leroy challenged.

"I guess maybe I'll have to show you how it's done," she replied.

"I don't think you can do it."

"Be serious! I can shoot a gun," Elizabeth argued.

"Sure you can shoot a gun but can you hit anything?" Leroy asked. "There's a lot more to hunting than you think."

"Oh please! Such as what?"

"Well, first you have to sight in your gun, then you have to practice hitting the target. Then there's learning how to walk quietly, sit patiently for hours and, maybe, you will see a deer. Then, of course, there's always the chance you could get buck fever and miss it completely."

Elizabeth laughed. "I think you're just trying to get me to back out now."

"Elizabeth," Mom scolded. "Hunting is not for girls."

"Aw Mom, women hunted back in pioneer days," Elizabeth disagreed.

Mom laughed. "These are not pioneer days. Besides you are too old to be acting like a tomboy."

"Just think of how much more meat we'd have," Elizabeth coaxed.

When Dad came in some minutes later he sided with Elizabeth.

"I think she can do it," he said.

Mom's protests were all to no avail. And so after supper, Leroy gave Elizabeth her first lesson in target practicing.

"You're serious, aren't you?" Matthew chuckled when Elizabeth told him about her bet with Leroy.

"Why, don't you think I can do it either?" asked Elizabeth.

Matthew shrugged. "I think you can probably do almost anything you set your mind to," he said. One thing he had learned about her in these past several months was how determined she was.

"When are you leaving for your hunting trip to Colorado?" asked Elizabeth.

"Three weeks from tomorrow, I sure wish I could take you along." He hugged her close. "Maybe someday just the two of us can go."

"How long will you be gone?" she asked.

"Four weeks. Some of the guys gave up going because their girlfriends didn't like it. I guess they didn't trust them."

Elizabeth nodded. She knew who some of the girls were.

"Do you trust me?" Matthew asked.

"I don't think I'd agreed to go steady with you if I didn't," she answered.

"I'm glad you feel that way. I think I'm the luckiest guy in the world." Leaning over toward her, he kissed her tenderly. "I love you," he whispered.

Elizabeth returned the kiss. "I love you too."

"What are you doing with your free weekends now that Matthew isn't here?" asked Dena.

Elizabeth shrugged. "Reading, taking walks with Marilyn. I missed him Sunday."

"That's good," said Dena. "I heard some of the boys had to give up their trip because the girls couldn't make it without them?"

"Yes, that's true," Elizabeth said.

"I know lots of the couples dating are also sleeping together," said Dena. "I wish more would get preached on the importance of a pure courtship."

"Surely they know its wrong to sleep together!"

"True," agreed Dena, "but just the same I think they should be taught how to resist the temptation. Our bodies are the temple of the Lord and it's so important to keep ourselves pure before Him."

Elizabeth was quiet. Dena had given her a lot to think about. She knew she and Matthew had done their share of kissing, but it would never go farther than that!

"Today is the big day!" said Leroy smiling broadly. He and Elizabeth hurried to finish the chores so they could be on their way before daylight.

"Are you sure you are up for this?" he teased as they checked their guns.

"You bet!" said Elizabeth hoping Leroy didn't know her stomach was full of butterflies.

She listened carefully as her brother gave her several last minute instructions, including how to find the tree stand and what to do first in the event that she should be lucky enough to get a deer.

"Just be careful," he warned as they slipped into their orange hunting vests and headed for the woods.

Walking along in the dark, Elizabeth shivered, partly from the cold and partly from nervousness. There had been a hard frost the night before causing her feet to make a soft crunching sound in the grass beneath her feet as she walked.

Several minutes later she arrived at the tree stand. Taking a deep breath and placing her gun in the proper position, she climbed up to her perch.

The cold morning air was invigorating and Elizabeth enjoyed watching the sun slowly began to rise. She wondered if maybe somewhere way out west Matthew was hunting too, maybe even watching the same sun rising. The thought was incomprehensible to her.

What an awesome creator their God was! The birds chirped cheerfully as the sun rose higher in the sky.

Elizabeth looked at her little pocket watch. Thirty minutes had passed. In the distance she heard gunshots being fired. Her heart beat a little faster. Maybe she would see something too.

Just then several does came crashing through the little clearing. Elizabeth jumped up, almost falling out of the tree stand, her heart pounding. "Better calm down," she said to herself, "or you'll never be able hold the gun steady." She watched as the deer disappeared through the trees. "This will calm me down," she said popping a piece of gum in her mouth.

Sinking down on the floor of the tree stand, she leaned back against the tree and listened to the squirrels and chipmunks scolding in the distance. A grouse flew up out of the bushes to her left. Elizabeth grinned, thinking how noisy the woods actually were.

The minutes seemed to drag on endlessly. She looked at her watch again. Only ten minutes had passed since the last time she had checked. Her leg felt like it had fallen asleep. She got up and slowly stretched. Then, taking a moment to look around, Elizabeth froze, her knees going weak. There, just beyond the clearing, was a big buck.

Ever so slowly she raised the gun to her right shoulder. Shutting her left eye, she pressed her right eye hard against the scope trying desperately to locate the deer in her sites. "Oh, there he is," she breathed a sigh of relief. Up and to the left a little she calculated, making sure she had the cross hairs on the center of his chest.

Placing her finger on the trigger, she pulled back hard. Bang! Everything went black for several seconds as Elizabeth sank to the ground.

"I must've shot myself, "she panicked. Dropping the gun, she placed her hand over her right eye, the source of her pain, trying to figure out what had gone wrong.

Suddenly, she realized what had occurred. Her head had been too close to the scope when she shot and, being a shotgun, it had kicked, causing the scope to hit her eye.

Forgetting all about the deer, Elizabeth leaned back against the tree. How funny she must've looked! Elizabeth laughed, glad no one had been around to see her.

"Oh no, where is the deer?" she said aloud. Jumping up she looked around. "Oh well," she said to herself, "I guess I missed it." Her legs felt shaky as she made her way down the tree. "Might as well go home. I've had enough excitement for one day."

"It wasn't as easy as I had thought it would be," she said to herself, "but I can't let Leroy know that!" She headed toward home.

About fifty yards from the tree, Elizabeth came across a dead deer. "It's my deer," she said excitedly, running up to take a closer look. "I didn't miss after all! I'd better go get Dad or Leroy to help me." Then she stopped. "I'm supposed to do something," she thought. Then she remembered, "Oh yes, cut it somewhere, and tag it, that's what Leroy said. Oh well, it'll only take me ten minutes to get home. I'll do it first thing when I get back." She ran toward the farm.

"I got him!" she called excitedly to Leroy, as she spotted him heading across the lawn.

"Yeah, right!' he answered.

"No, really, I did it!" she gasped, running up to him. "Come help me get him home."

"Really? Way to go!" Leroy laughed. "Where is it? Did you tag it?"

"He's back by the clearing."

"You shot a buck?" Leroy asked in surprise.

Elizabeth nodded.

"Are you sure?" he sounded disbelieving.

"I may have been excited but I know horns when I see them," said Elizabeth sarcastically.

"Antlers, they are called antlers," said Leroy, following Elizabeth out to the barn to get the horse and cart out.

"Okay, whatever," she threw over her shoulder as she kept walking.

"Hey, wait a minute," Leroy stopped. "What happened to your eye?"

"Aw, it's nothing," she hedged, feeling embarrassed at the foolish mistake she'd made. "Come on, let's go get the deer."

"Where'd you have the gun when you shot?" he asked.

"Don't worry about it," Elizabeth replied. "I got the deer, didn't I?" She hoped he would drop the subject but, upon hearing his hearty laugh as she walked away, she knew she would never hear the end of it.

"What a beauty!" Leroy whistled through his teeth as he looked down at the deer. "A ten pointer at that!"

"Is that good?" asked Elizabeth excitedly.

"You bet it is," said Leroy proudly. "The biggest one I ever got was an eight pointer."

Between the two of them they soon had the deer field dressed and returned home.

"Elizabeth!" Mom gasped as they entered the house. "What happened to your eye?"

Elizabeth groaned, knowing she'd have to give a full account of her accident before Mom would be satisfied.

"Don't feel too bad," Dad comforted when she finished her story. "I'd be willing to suffer a black eye for a trophy like that. You did a good job," he said proudly.

Elizabeth spent the next two days helping to butcher the deer, cut up the meat and can it. "This is a good experience for you," said Mom as she instructed Elizabeth with the canning. "You have to know these things when you get married."

Elizabeth laughed, "I'm not getting married just yet."

"I know that's what you think," said Mom. "But the time will be here before you know it." Mom knew most Amish girls were capable of running the house by themselves by the time they were sixteen or seventeen. They were taught to sew, cook, clean, and can, and all the other necessary things that went along with running a home. Mom felt confident that Elizabeth would do okay. She wasn't afraid of hard work, and it certainly was hard work to live on a farm and raise a big family. "Yah, God has been good to us, blessing us with good obedient children."

Chapter Seventeen

"Elizabeth, would you go get the mail?" called Mom from the living room.

Slipping into her coat Elizabeth dashed across the lawn. "A letter for me," she smiled recognizing Matthew's handwriting.

Hurrying back to the house, she dropped the rest of the mail in Mom's lap and hurried upstairs to the privacy of her bedroom to read her long-awaited letter.

Dearest Elizabeth,

Wonder how this finds you? I am having the time of my life! It's even more beautiful here than I'd remembered. I wish you were here! I will wait until I return home to tell you about my hunting stories. I wonder if you will have one to tell me? I can hardly wait to see you again. I plan to come home next Friday evening, so I'm hoping I can come early Sunday so we can spend the whole day together. If that doesn't suit you, let me know.

Miss you, Love you,
Matthew

Elizabeth read the letter several times, picturing Matthew's smile. Next Sunday seemed like an eternity away. He had been gone almost a month and she could hardly wait to see him!

Sunday morning finally came. Traditionally the Amish only attended church every two weeks. Today was the Hostetler's Sunday off, so chores were done later and then there were family devotions and a big brunch followed.

Elizabeth took great care getting dressed wanting to look her best for Matthew. Then she heard Dad's voice from downstairs saying, "Come on in." She suddenly felt nervous. This was the first time Matthew had come to spend a Sunday like this with her family. She wondered if he felt nervous too. She knew she would be if she had to go to his house. But upon entering the living room and hearing Dad and Matthew deep in conversation about his trip, she knew she needn't have worried.

Matthew looked up when she entered the room. "Hi," he smiled warmly, wishing he could get up and take her in his arms.

"Hi," Elizabeth replied. "Did you have a good trip?" She sat down on the couch next to him.

"Yes, but I was ready to come home."

Just then Mom poked her head around the corner. "Brunch is on," she said.

Soon everyone gathered around the table to eat biscuits, gravy, sausage, fried potatoes, and fried mush. Elizabeth loved their Sunday brunches, and this particular meal was her favorite.

Elizabeth nodded. "The Bible says if we confess our sins He is faithful to forgive us. He took everyone of your sins on Him when he died on the cross for you and me."

"How do I know for sure?"

Elizabeth jumped up. "I'll be right back," she said.

She quickly returned, Bible in hand. Flipping through the pages she opened it to 1 John 5:13 and read aloud, "These things have I written that ye may know that ye have eternal life." All you have to do is ask Him to forgive you," she told Cathy earnestly, "and trust in His blood to wash away your sins. That's why He came."

The tears in Cathy's eyes were now spilling down her cheeks. "How do you know all this?"

"Rachel told me," Elizabeth said. She told Cathy all about Rachel and how they had both asked Jesus to come into their hearts and wash away their sins.

"Did you feel different after you prayed?" asked Cathy.

Elizabeth nodded. "It's hard to put into words but I felt clean and free. I guess it's like the Bible says in John, 'You shall know the truth and the truth shall set you free.' And that's how I felt, free of all the fear and guilt."

"I would like to feel that way too," said Cathy through her tears.

And that afternoon, underneath the old oak tree, it felt to Elizabeth as if heaven came down when Cathy prayed a simple prayer asking God to forgive her and for Jesus to come into her heart. Elizabeth remembered that the Bible talked about the angels in heaven rejoicing over one sinner that repented and was born into the family of God. She wondered if Rachel was among those rejoicing at the throne of God.

Elizabeth clenched her hands nervously in her lap. Today was the day she would be baptized. She and the five others in the membership class were given a special seat in front of the congregation. Knowing that all eyes were upon them, she tried to sit up a little straighter and concentrate on the sermon.

As Bishop Joe talked about the damnation that awaited those who left the church, Elizabeth felt a chill go up her spine. There was that dreaded shunning thing. It was hard for her to understand how a group of people who showed so much love and compassion in times of crisis could shun so coldly. She wished she could understand it better. How could it be right? The Bible said God is love.

She listened as the bishop went on to talk about being an upbuilding member of the church and saying no to temptation.

"Oh, Lord," Elizabeth prayed silently. "Help me to always shine as light for you, and to love others the way you love me."

The class was then asked to kneel, whereupon the bishop's wife removed Cathy and Elizabeth's coverings.

Bishop Joe began with the boys, placing his hands on their heads, asking all the traditional questions, and sprinkling water over their heads. Then it was the girls' turn.

Elizabeth felt nervous as Bishop Joe stepped in front of her and asked the first question.

"Can you confess with the Eunuch that Jesus Christ is the Son of God?" he asked in a solemn voice.

"Yes," she answered, keeping her eyes averted.

"Do you also confess this to be a Christian doctrine church and brotherhood to which you are about to submit?"

Again she answered with yes.

Bishop Joe cleared his throat and continued. "Do you renounce the world and the devil and his evil lusts as well as your own flesh and blood desires, to serve only Jesus Christ who died on the cross for you?"

To this Elizabeth gladly answered yes.

The bishop then asked the last question. "Do you also promise in the presence of God and His church with the Lord's help to support these doctrines, rules and regulations, to earnestly fill your place in the church, to help counsel and labor and not depart from this doctrine, come what may, life or death?"

Again Elizabeth answered with a yes.

Bishop Joe then sprinkled the water over her head saying, "I baptize you in the name of the Father, Son and Holy Spirit."

The bishop's wife then placed the covering back on Elizabeth's head and helped her to her to feet, greeting her with the holy kiss.

Elizabeth's legs felt a bit shaky. She could hardly believe she was now a member of the Amish church.

"I'll bet you're glad it's over with," said Matthew, as they headed home from the singing that evening.

"Yes, I sure am," said Elizabeth. "I was pretty nervous, I was afraid I'd mess up or something."

"I remember the feeling," said Matthew. "But aren't you glad you did it?"

"I guess so but, at the same time, it's such a big responsibility making all those promises," said Elizabeth.

"I guess I never thought about those things when I got baptized," he admitted. Then he changed the subject to one closer to his heart.

"Did your parents have any objections to us setting a wedding date for next summer?" asked Matthew.

"No they didn't," answered Elizabeth. "Did you say anything to your parents?"

Matthew nodded. "They love you," he said. "They're happy to add you to the family."

"Did you have a date in mind?" Elizabeth asked.

"I think June would be nice," Matthew replied. "What do you think?"

"Let's look at the calendar when we get home," decided Elizabeth.

"I'm running into town this afternoon," said Leroy, poking his head into the kitchen. "Do you need anything?"

"Yes, I could use a few things," said Mom. "I'll make a list."

"Can I go along and get dropped off at Cathy's house, then you could pick me up on your way home?" Elizabeth asked.

"You girls are always trying to find a way to get together," muttered Leroy.

"Can I, Mom?" begged Elizabeth, ignoring Leroy's remark. "It's her birthday today and I have a gift to give her."

"Okay," Mom told her, happy to see that Elizabeth had finally made another best friend since Rachel's death.

"So have you set a date for your wedding?" asked Leroy, once they were on their way to town.

Elizabeth nodded. "June sixteenth."

"I can hardly believe my little sister is getting married." Leroy shook his head.

"What about you?" asked Elizabeth. "Has Miss Right come along yet?"

"Maybe."

"It's Cathy, isn't it?" asked Elizabeth.

"What do you think?"

"I don't think you could find a nicer girl," said Elizabeth sincerely.

"I feel kinda awkward asking her out," Leroy admitted. "I mean, I don't want to make her uncomfortable since I spend a lot of time there helping with the farm work. She has turned several guys down. Why would I be any different?"

"Well, for starters I think you are already friends, right?"

Leroy nodded.

"And you are way cuter than those other guys," teased Elizabeth.

"Keep talking," Leroy grinned.

Elizabeth turned serious. "I think if you pray and if you feel at peace about it, then ask her," she advised.

"I get nervous just thinking about it," admitted Leroy. "I just wish I knew how she felt."

"There's only one way to find out," Elizabeth said. "You gotta ask her."

"What a nice surprise!" said Cathy meeting Elizabeth at the door.

"Happy birthday." Elizabeth handed her a package.

"Oh, this is so nice," said Cathy, holding up a miniature cedar chest. "You shouldn't have."

"Well, that's one reason I came over, but there's another one," Elizabeth admitted. "I was wondering if I could borrow some patterns?"

"I won't even ask," laughed Cathy, bringing out a box of patterns from the bedroom.

"That's okay," smiled Elizabeth. "You're my best friend. I can tell you the date. It's June sixteenth." She hesitated, then asked, "How about you? You're twenty now. Is getting married your dream?"

Cathy's smile disappeared. "I'll never get married," she said quietly.

"Why do you say that?" asked Elizabeth curiously.

"Well, remember when I told you I had sinned and did things I knew better than to do?" she asked.

Elizabeth nodded.

Cathy went on. "Back in Indiana I had a boyfriend. We had an improper relationship, and at first I felt guilty, but all the romance books I read made it seem so right. I mean we were going to get married someday anyway, I convinced myself. And if we were in love then how could it be wrong?" Cathy shook her head regretfully.

"Then one day my sister invited me to attend a special meeting at her church and I went. A lady was teaching about love and relationships. She talked about keeping ourselves pure, and about waiting until marriage. Then she held up a paper heart that was beautifully decorated and said this was our heart, but if we were impure in our relationships with our boyfriends it was like giving him a piece of our heart. She then took a scissors and cut off a piece of the heart. I began to see where she was going.

"By the time she finished," Cathy went on, "she was holding up a pathetic looking piece of paper, saying, 'How will you feel to offer this to the man that God has chosen for you to marry?'

"I felt so bad when I was faced with my sin, I knew I couldn't go on living like that any longer. So I decided the next time my boyfriend and I got together, I would tell him all about it and then we would change our ways together."

"What happened?"

"To make a long story short, he didn't agree with me. So we parted ways, and six months later he had to marry another girl." She shook her head at the painful memories. "So you see, I can never get married," she concluded.

"But God has forgiven you," Elizabeth reminded her. "The Bible says in Hebrews that He forgives us and remembers our sin no more. That means there's no record of it because the blood of Jesus washed it away."

"Yes I know God forgave me," Cathy said. "But I know no decent guy would want me if they knew. You know what they call a girl like me?" Not waiting for an answer, she went on, "used goods, that's what!" She wiped away her tears.

"I decided after that that I would never again get involved with a guy," she continued. "I couldn't bear to have anyone know such a shameful thing about me, but now, well, I've fallen in love with someone, and I can't bear the thought of having to tell him my story and see the rejection in his eyes."

"But what if this guy you're in love with is in love with you too?" asked Elizabeth.

"I would tell him no, then go and nurse my broken heart," sighed Cathy.

"Please don't do that!" said Elizabeth. "Because I know it would break his heart too, and he would never know why he was refused. I've seen the way you act around guys and I would have to say you act better than any of the other girls around here. You are my best friend, and nothing you tell me will change that."

"Thank you for the things you said," replied Cathy. "I'm glad you're still my friend after all the things you know about me. I wish I could go back and change everything but I can't and now I will have a lifetime of regret because of my past."

Elizabeth thought about her conversation with Cathy that week as she went about her work. Was she as pure in her relationship with Matthew as she should be? The question went around and around in her head. She knew she wouldn't rest until she had an answer.

Getting her Bible she walked back to her favorite place in the woods where she liked to come and be alone. Reading verse after verse, she thought about what Mom had said. Love wasn't just a feeling. Sometimes young people mistook infatuation for love. Read 1 Corinthians 13 she had told Elizabeth, so Elizabeth read it now. When she finished, she began to understand that true love was unselfish; it was all about putting others first.

Closing her Bible, she sat deep in thought. She would have to tell Matthew how she felt—about everything.

"Oh Lord," she prayed. "Please forgive me for not being pure in my thoughts and actions toward Matthew. Help me to keep myself pure before you, and walk in your ways. Help me to tell Matthew how I really feel."

Elizabeth's heart felt much lighter as she walked toward home. She knew that doing the right thing wouldn't be easy but she knew that was better than a lifetime of regret.

"You're awfully quiet today," observed Matthew as they sat down on the porch swing. "Did I say or do something wrong?"

Elizabeth shook her head. She knew the moment of truth had come. "I have some things I need to tell you," she confessed, "and I don't really know where to start."

"You can tell me anything," Matthew encouraged, taking her hand in his.

His tenderness brought tears to her eyes. This man would be her husband in a few short months, and she had never trusted him enough to tell him the things that mattered most to her. Little by little, through her tears, Elizabeth told him how she felt. She began by telling him all about Rachel and how they always wanted to know if they were going to heaven. She told him how they had prayed and asked Jesus to come into their heart, and how she believed that her name was written in heaven.

Matthew sat quietly listening to every word she said. "I don't know what to say," he replied when she was done. "You know the Amish teach that you can't know whether or not you are going to heaven; you can only hope. I'm ashamed to say that I don't read my Bible enough to tell you if that's right or not. But I would like for you to show me those verses so we could talk about it."

Elizabeth smiled. "I would love that more than anything. But there's something else I need to talk to you about," she went on, feeling a bit embarrassed. "It's about being pure in our courtship," she said blushing. "I've been thinking a lot about how far is too far for unmarried couples, and then I began looking in the Bible for answers. I didn't find any verse that gave me an exact answer," she admitted, "but the Bible does talk about the lust of the flesh and about staying pure. Then I read Ephesians 5:27 where it says 'That He might present it to Himself a glorious church [bride] not having spot or wrinkle, or any such thing but that it should be holy and without blemish.' I love you, Matthew, and I want to be pure for you."

"Say no more, you sweet thing," said Matthew, squeezing her hand. "I'm sorry, I should be the one to set a standard for our relationship. Today you have put me to shame in how much more you know than me, but if we can make a fresh new start, I would like for us to do things differently."

Matthew took both her hands in his. "Promise me that you won't ever keep anything from me or be afraid to tell me anything again?"

"I promise," Elizabeth said. "I want God's blessing to be on our marriage."

After Matthew left, Elizabeth breathed a prayer of thanks. She felt closer to him than she ever had before, and was glad they were going to work together on heading in the right direction.

Chapter Twenty-Two

"We need to plan a time to go shopping for all the wedding stuff," Mom said to Elizabeth as they finished washing the dishes. "Did you have a time in mind?"

"No," Elizabeth replied, "but I was hoping we could go on a Saturday so Marilyn could go along." She and Marilyn had become much closer ever since they'd apologized to each other. In fact, just the week before Marilyn had confided in her that Steven had proposed marriage.

"Let's plan on going next Saturday then," said Mom, "if it's okay with Marilyn."

Marilyn and Elizabeth could hardly wait until the weekend. A shopping trip was a rare thing. This one would take most of the day.

"Do you know what shade of blue you are going to choose for your wedding dress?" asked Marilyn.

Elizabeth shook her head, "No, but we will have fun deciding." Blue was the traditional color for an Amish bride. She knew she could pick the shade and the material but she knew, too, that Mom would have the final vote.

"My feet feel like they are going to fall off," said Marilyn, on their way home Saturday night.

"Me, too," agreed Elizabeth. "But it's worth it." she grinned. They had gone to three stores before they found just the right shade of blue, then there were shoes to buy and organdy for the cape and apron. What a day! In between, they had had lunch at a restaurant. Elizabeth had enjoyed every second of that rare experience. She could count the times she'd eaten at a restaurant, and could hardly wait to tell Matthew all about it!

"How did the shopping go yesterday?" asked Matthew, thinking he already knew the answer by Elizabeth's pleased smile.

"It was so much fun," Elizabeth told him all about their day.

"Well, I did some shopping this week too," he said, presenting her with a package.

Elizabeth looked surprised. Opening the package she pulled out a book. "*Building on the Right Foundation,*" she read. "This is so nice."

"I just thought we could use some help," said Matthew. "I'm sure there's a lot I need to learn about marriage. I got us each one," he added. "I thought we could both read it during the week, then discuss it on the weekend and maybe that would help us stay on the right track."

Elizabeth opened the book. "Look what it says here: 'For no other foundation can anyone lay than that which is laid, which is Jesus Christ—1 Corinthians 3:11.' That is so fitting," she said. "I'm sure we will learn a lot."

Matthew nodded, "I've already read the first chapter and I can tell you I had no idea there was so much to learn about."

"I couldn't resist these either," he grinned, handing her several more books by her favorite author.

"Oh Matthew, you shouldn't have—but I'm glad you did! I guess you know what I like."

"I'm learning," Matthew said, then he added, "I have some more good news. We are going to start on the plans for our house. I have a couple ready which I'll bring along next week so you can tell me what you like best."

"I don't know anything about that kind of stuff," admitted Elizabeth, "I'm sure I'll be happy however you make it."

"That's what I love about you," said Matthew. "You are so easy going, but I'm afraid I have to warn you that I'm not."

Elizabeth couldn't imagine Matthew getting upset, but she knew it would just be part of really getting to know one another and that, she thought, is a good thing.

"Where are you off to?" asked Elizabeth seeing Leroy hitch up his horse.

"To help the Schrocks husk corn," he answered.

Elizabeth smiled. "Cornfields in the fall are pretty romantic."

"That's what I'm counting on," said Leroy before driving away.

"Hi, Leroy," Andy greeted him with a hearty smile. "Are you ready to husk corn?"

"Ready as I'll ever be," he grinned. "Why the two wagons? Is someone else coming to help?"

"Cathy and our cousin Leona agreed to help today," Andy replied and, as if on cue, the two girls appeared.

"Hi there," they greeted. "We're ready to go," said Cathy.

"Leona, you can go with me," Andy directed, "and Cathy can go with Leroy."

Leroy could hardly believe his good fortune. Maybe today would be the day he could tell Cathy how he felt about her.

"It's a perfect day for corn husking," said Cathy. "Fall is my favorite time of the year."

"Me too," agreed Leroy. "I think the air even feels special somehow."

The two of them made small talk as they rode out to the field.

"Let me know when you get ready to take a break," said Leroy, as they began husking corn.

Soon a steady thud, thud sound filled the air as the two worked tossing ear after ear of corn into the empty wagon.

"How can I tell her?" worried Leroy. "What if she doesn't feel the same as I do?" He glanced over where she was busily working. Their eyes met and Cathy smiled at him.

"I'll tell her the first opportunity," he vowed to himself. An hour later he had his chance.

"Are you ready for a break?" called Cathy.

"I'd say it's about that time," Leroy looked at his watch. "It's ten o'clock."

"It feels more like twelve o'clock to my wrists," said Cathy.

"Here, let me give you a hand." Leroy reached down to help her up. Sinking down on the wagon floor she began rubbing her tired wrists. "Thanks for coming to help me." she said. "I just can't seem to keep up with you, I'm afraid I'm not making a very good working partner."

Leroy sat down beside her. "I don't agree with that," he said. "I like very much having you for a working partner."

Cathy looked up to find Leroy's eyes upon her. Her heart skipped a beat at his tender look.

"There's something I've been wanting to talk to you about for a long time," he said, not taking his eyes off hers. "I would like us to be more than just friends."

Cathy felt as if her heart would burst with happiness. He felt the same way she did! But just as quickly her heart sank. The moment of truth had come; she would have to tell him. "Oh, Lord, give me the strength to tell him the truth," she prayed silently.

"I'm sorry if I've offended you," said Leroy, seeing her subdued look.

"It's not that," Cathy shook her head. "I just don't think I'm the girl you think I am." Seeing his confused look she went on. "When I was seventeen I had a boyfriend and, well, I'm not a ..." She couldn't bring herself to go on. "I'm sorry but it wouldn't be fair not to tell you. No guy wants a girl that hasn't kept herself pure," she said through her tears.

Leroy felt his heart sink at her news, but seeing her tears was more than he could bear.

Reaching out to her, he pulled her into his arms and held her as she cried. "It's okay," he said. "Your past is part of who you are today, and it's part of what makes you who you are. I wouldn't be honest to say I wasn't disappointed, but it's who you are today that I've fallen in love with."

"Are you saying you still want me?" Cathy asked, surprised.

Leroy nodded, pulling her close and hugging her. This time Cathy responded by hugging him back.

"You still haven't given me an answer," Leroy said looking down at her.

Blushing, Cathy smiled. "I must confess you have been about all I've been able to think of for quite some time."

"Does that mean I can come to see you for an official date on Sunday then?" Leroy asked.

Looking up at him, she said. "Maybe you should take some time to think about it. I don't think I could bear it if you would change your mind later on."

"Everyone makes mistakes," Leroy said gently. "I didn't just ask you on a whim. I've prayed about this and felt like it was God's will for me to ask you. I want us to get to know one another in the hopes of becoming husband and wife."

"I don't deserve you," said Cathy humbly.

"Wait till you get to know me before you say that," he smiled mischievously.

Cathy laughed. "I can hardly wait to get to know you then."

Leroy glanced over at her, thinking he'd never seen her look sweeter. Resisting the urge to take her in his arms and kiss her, he got to his feet. "I reckon we'd best get back to work before the others come to find us," he smiled.

Leroy thought about their conversation as he went on husking corn. He was glad he had told her how he felt and equally glad she returned his love. He thought about how much he'd wanted to take her in his arms and kiss her, she had looked so sweet. But he knew that was not his right yet. He knew that if he waited until it was his right and she belonged to him, it would be sweeter still.

Chapter Twenty-Three

"I just have to tell you I never thought I could be this happy," Cathy said to Elizabeth as they sat on the porch swing.

"Well, I'm guessing if Leroy's smile is anything to go by, I'd say he feels the same way," Elizabeth responded. "I couldn't be happier for both of you."

"I know it's only been a month that we've been dating," said Cathy, "but it seems like we've known each other for ages. It's so different this time. We talk and laugh together and are really getting to know each other. I know now I didn't really love my last boyfriend. When too much touching is involved, you go by what you feel and never learn the meaning of true love."

Elizabeth nodded. "I know. We have learned that the hard way too," she said. "Remember the day you told me about your past?" she asked.

Cathy nodded.

"Well, I went home and did some serious thinking." She told Cathy about how she had talked to Matthew. Our relationship is so much better now," she concluded. "I feel closer and more in love with him than I did before."

"I know what you mean," Cathy agreed. "I feel like God has given me a second chance and I want to make sure I keep myself pure so that His blessings can be on us."

"I can hardly believe it's almost Christmas already," said Elizabeth, as she and Marilyn worked at making the last of the pies for Christmas day. "Time is going by too fast. I just want to enjoy my last few months at home, because I know once I leave things will never be the same. I won't be a little girl anymore. I won't be the daughter of David and Mary Hostetler, I'll be the wife of Matthew Yoder."

Marilyn laughed. "You are always so dramatic! Me? I can't wait to have my own house and set my dishes and other things in my cupboards."

Elizabeth smiled. "Yah, I know what you mean. When I think of that, it sounds exciting to me too. But just the same, I feel as if a precious time in our lives is slipping away."

Listening to the girls' conversation from the living room, Mom wiped the tears from her eyes. How she wished they could stay her little girls forever. Her heart ached with sadness knowing the last of their three children would soon be gone. It seemed not so long ago they were all at home and her life had been so busy trying to care for them all. "Oh Lord," she prayed, "we have done the best we knew in bringing them up right. Please help me learn to let go and trust them to your care because they really belong to you."

"Only two more weeks until the wedding!" Elizabeth said as she and Matthew worked packing up her belongings.

"Yes, I thought when we started building the house we'd have plenty of time," Matthew replied, "but here it is June already and its still not done."

"Will it be ready for us to move into the day after the wedding?"

"It should be. My brothers are all helping me to finish it this week."

"You still have time to back out though," Elizabeth teased.

"I do?" he threw back.

Elizabeth looked at the calendar. "Oh no, I'm sorry. Yesterday was the last day to cancel." Matthew reached over and grabbed her hand. "I love you," he said softly.

"I love you too," Elizabeth replied. "I just hope you're planning on helping me keep my head together through this wedding."

Matthew knew Elizabeth got nervous easily. "Remember," he advised, "just take one thing at a time and you'll be fine."

As the wedding day drew closer Elizabeth tried to remember what Matthew had told her and she tried to remain calm. But every time she turned around, there seemed to be another dilemma that required her attention.

"We are sure going to miss having you around," said Dena, as the sisters all worked together around one table making pies.

"I'm going to miss you all too," said Elizabeth.

"I don't think you've ever told us your and Matthew's love story," said Anna. "I would like to hear it."

Elizabeth felt embarrassed. "I don't—"

Luckily she was interrupted by Cathy's arrival.

"Hi Cathy," welcomed Linda. "You may as well come over here and see what all's involved in getting ready for a wedding."

Cathy went over to the table, feeling thankful for this family who so readily accepted her and made her feel a part of them.

"Yes," Marilyn said, "Elizabeth was just getting ready to tell us about when she and Matthew fell in love."

"Oh no!" Elizabeth groaned. "I thought I'd gotten out of it."

"Not that easy," said Dena.

"I'll tell my story only if you all agree to tell yours," she bargained.

After everyone had agreed, Elizabeth began.

"The first time I remember seeing Matthew was at your house, Anna, the night of Daniel's birthday party. That night he winked at me and I thought he was kinda wicked.

"The next time I saw him he was so sweet to me I started liking him." Elizabeth remembered back to that summer day when Matthew had so tenderly wrapped up her injured arm.

"Then what happened?" asked Linda.

"Well," Elizabeth continued, "once again we were both at Daniel's helping them butcher and that day he kissed me for the first time."

"You wicked girl," teased Anna. "I know when you are talking about. Why, you weren't even sixteen yet!"

Elizabeth blushed. "I know; I was afraid he would think I was just that kind of girl and never speak to me again. It wasn't until after I was sixteen that I saw him again, this time in town. He was in the process of asking me on a date when Nancy came along and interrupted him. Then that weekend he left for Montana and it wasn't until after my accident that I saw him again."

"Is that when he asked you?" interrupted Dena.

Elizabeth shook her head. "A couple weeks later he wrote me a letter and the rest is history," she finished.

One by one the rest took turns sharing their stories. Elizabeth looked around the table at her sisters, enjoying the moment. "Oh Lord," she prayed, "help me to never take my family for granted."

"Are you ready?" asked Matthew.

"Yes, I'll be down in a minute," Elizabeth called back. It was the night before the wedding and Matthew was taking her to town for pizza.

"Did you see the wedding cake?" asked Elizabeth.

Matthew nodded. "It's beautiful."

The four-tiered cake had been done all in white. Elizabeth stood back to admire the tiny rosebuds and the shell edging. She had chosen navy and burgundy to decorate the bride and groom's table. The best china and silverware had been used. The candy bowls that graced the table were of blue carnival glass, as was the punch bowl. The fresh flowers were deep red velvet roses.

"It looks like a dream," said Matthew.

Elizabeth nodded. "I think it is," she smiled.

"I guess this is kinda like our last date," commented Elizabeth as they drove into town.

"I guess I'll have to make a date with you at least once a month after we're married," said Matthew. "That book talked about taking time and doing special things to keep the romance alive in your marriage."

Elizabeth loved the warm and intimate look he gave her. "I feel like I've learned so much from reading that book," she said. "But the one thing I want to try and remember is where it said that your happiness should come from what you can do for your partner and not just in what your partner does for you."

Chapter Twenty-Four

June sixteenth dawned bright and clear with not a cloud in the sky. "The perfect day for a wedding," thought Elizabeth, hurrying up to her room to get dressed for the ceremony and hoping to find time for a few minutes alone.

She pulled her wedding dress from the closet and laid it carefully on the bed, then she sat down in front of her mirror and picked up her comb. Satisfied at last that every hair was neatly in place, she started to retrieve her covering from her dresser when spotted a white envelope, attached to a long stemmed pink rose.

Elizabeth recognized Matthew's handwriting. Sitting on the edge of her bed, she opened the envelope and took out the card.

Dearest Elizabeth,

Wherever you go, I will go; wherever you lodge, I will lodge; your people shall be my people and your God, my God. Ruth 1:16.

May we always be as happy as we are today.
Love,
Matthew

Elizabeth wiped away a tear, her heart touched by Matthew's thoughtfulness. Getting up from the bed she pinned on her covering, taking one last look in the mirror to make sure it was properly pinned in place. "You'll be a married woman in a couple hours," she said aloud, the words sounding strange to her ears.

Hearing a knock at the door she turned around. "Come in," she called.

"Do you think it would be okay if I came in to steal a kiss from my bride?" Matthew peeked in the door.

"Could I refuse you when you look so devastatingly handsome?"

"You are the most beautiful bride I've ever seen," Matthew said, kissing her softly.

"Thank you for the card and the rose."

"Are you two about ready to go?" Leroy came to the door.

"Yes, I think so," said Matthew. "I wanted to tell you to make sure you watch and listen closely today, Leroy, so you will know what to do or not to do when your turn comes."

"I will," Leroy agreed. "October isn't all that far away."

"Leroy Hostetler!" exclaimed Elizabeth. "Are you serious?"

Leroy laughed at her response. "I'm old enough, aren't I?"

"Congratulations, old buddy," said Matthew, shaking his hand. "There for a while I thought you might end up a lonely old bachelor."

Cathy entered the room just in time to hear Matthew's teasing.

"He might have if I wouldn't have taken pity on him," she said laughingly.

Elizabeth laughed too. "Well Leroy, I think you've met your match," she declared.

"I think God gave me the perfect match," he said, smiling tenderly at Cathy.

At the church, Elizabeth tried to sit perfectly still and listen to each word of instruction given to them by the officiating bishop. She listened as he told the story of Adam and Eve and talked about the covenant between a husband and wife. After many instructions, he then asked them to come forward.

Joining their hands together, he took them through the wedding vows. "Do you promise to love and honor one another, for better or worse, through sickness and health, till death do you part?"

Answering yes to each of the questions, Matthew and Elizabeth were then pronounced man and wife.

Walking back to take their seats until the ceremony was over, Elizabeth felt strange. She was now Mrs. Elizabeth Yoder. She glanced at her new husband to find his eyes upon her.

Reaching over and clasping his hand, Elizabeth closed her eyes and prayed, "Oh Lord, thank you for Matthew. Help me to be the kind of wife you want me to be. Let my smile be the sunshine in his rainy days. Help to be an encourager to Matthew, bringing out the best in him. Lord, help us to stay close to you and daily walk hand in hand with you. Only you know what the future holds. Keep your hand upon us and lead us in the way everlasting. Amen."